LINGER

Edward Fallon

#3

Reckoning
for the
Damned

BRAUN HAUS MEDIA, LLC

*The publisher wishes to acknowledge
and thank Tim Tresslar
for his contribution to this work*

Sign up for the
Braun Haus Media, LLC Newsletter
and get a free ebook.

Yes, that's right.
A free full-length supernatural thriller
from our growing library of books.

Find out more at BraunHausMedia.com

Other books in the *Linger* series available for purchase now

#1
Dying is a Wild Night

#2
Trail of the Beast

#4
Here There Be Monsters

#5
The Death of Dreams

LINGER 3

Reckoning for the Damned

PART ONE

"One of the secrets of life is that all that is really worth doing is what we do for others."

~Lewis Carroll

1

THEY HADN'T BEEN IN FLORIDA thirty minutes before Kate Messenger discovered that an old acquaintance of hers had gone crazy outside Tallahassee, drove his car too fast, punched a cop, screamed about monsters and wound up in jail.

Then things fell apart.

Kate was in the passenger's seat of a '64 Rambler Cross Country as she and her two traveling companions hurtled east on Interstate 10, the Alabama state line in their rearview mirror.

Noah Weston was at the wheel, eyes fixed on the road, expression grim. From what he'd told Kate, the ancient station wagon had belonged to his late wife, a victim of the brutal killer they now hunted.

She didn't need her enhanced intuition to understand why

he'd kept it or what it represented to him. But until now, they had been riding separately and her experience with the LBJ-era death trap had thankfully been minimal.

After her SUV was torched, however, she'd had no choice but to join them, and had spent the last hour or so listening to it groan and rattle.

Christopher sat in the backseat, his sightless eyes fixed on some feature of the car's interior, oblivious to those around him. A small, pink photo album lay on the seat next to him, within arm's reach.

Kate had seen him like this a number of times now. The boy would lapse into what looked from the outside like a trance, quietly rocking back and forth in his seat. Though she still didn't understand it, she knew he was in the haze, doing whatever it was he did there.

Right now, she suspected he was searching for the girl whose name was scrawled in blue pen across the cover of the album: *Lucy*. The two had been in psychic communication until just a few hours ago and now Chris was worried that she was gone for good.

With him in the haze and Weston lost in his own thoughts, Kate had spent the time scrolling through the Internet with her cell phone, looking for information on a killer calling himself the Harbinger.

They'd heard news of him shortly after leaving Alabama, a brief bulletin on the Rambler's static-ridden radio that had piqued their interest, and Christopher had said they needed to head for Tallahassee.

Kate knew a harbinger was someone who traveled ahead, alerting people to the arrival of someone else. So far, however, this particular harbinger had only heralded murder. According to the media reports she'd found online, he had tortured and murdered at least three prostitutes in Florida and

Georgia, and investigators had found evidence that linked him to the disappearances of up to six more sex workers over the last several years.

That in and of itself hadn't warranted Kate's—or Weston's—attention. But, according to one source, the killer had sent a letter to a joint federal-state task force that had subsequently been leaked to the media. The letter contained taunts aimed at the task force and a couple of brief passages explaining the killer's desire to cleanse the earth of "whores" and "vermin."

He did it, he claimed, not because he was some crazed psychopath, but because he was performing a public service, like a garbage man.

Kate had heard those twisted rationalizations before, but they never failed to stoke a slow-burning rage inside her. Her mother had been murdered, the body left next to a Dumpster. Such cold disregard for life was something she couldn't abide, especially when the killer tried to put a positive spin on it.

That was all bad enough. More than enough to make her want to hunt the SOB down.

But it got worse.

At the bottom of the letter, the Harbinger had drawn a circle with a dot at the center, and that symbol—a circumpunct—had immediately caught her attention.

The serial murderer they had been hunting, the butcher they called the Beast, had that same symbol tattooed on his forearm.

So it looked as if Chris had been right about heading this way.

Now, Kate threw a glance at Weston, who'd been silent for at least an hour.

She could see his jaws clenched, small muscles rippling

under freshly shaved skin, eyebrows arched. The Beast had slaughtered his family, and in the process had nearly destroyed him.

He abruptly broke his silence. "How about we find a place to stay outside Tallahassee? Might save us a few bucks."

"Sounds like a plan," Kate said.

Weston nodded to her cell phone. "You find anything new on the Harbinger?"

"A couple articles quoting serial killer experts. Some quotes from neighbors about how scared they are with a murderer on the loose. The usual stuff."

"Nothing more about the circumpunct?"

"Not a thing. What do you make of it?"

Weston's brow furrowed. "I'm not sure. But from what you've told me, this guy doesn't work like the Beast. He's focused on hookers, and the Beast–"

"Will kill anyone."

"Right," Weston said. "And this one sent out a letter. That's not like the Beast, either. He's not one of these 'catch me before I kill again' killers. But I still have a bad feeling about this."

"Who wouldn't?"

"Not like that. The whole thing with the circumpunct is eating at me. This Harbinger creep has never shown it before, but right after we leave Alabama, his letter gets posted on the Internet."

"You think it's too coincidental."

"I think it bothers me. That's all. The Beast manipulated us in Singer. Who says he's not yanking our chains again?"

Kate gazed through the windshield, her eyes fixed on the road.

"The Harbinger could also be a fan," she said.

"A fan? Of the Beast?"

"Maybe fan's the wrong word. Fixated. There are people who are obsessed with serial killers and unsolved murders. They may not know of the Beast specifically, but they could know about the crimes. Maybe there's something written about the symbol somewhere."

"Well, the guy's not a crank. He's killed people."

Kate nodded. "He could've added the circumpunct as some kind of message to the Beast. An homage. A boast. Demanding attention. These are just guesses. It's not like I'm a profiler or anything."

Her phone pinged, alerting her that she'd received an email. She ran her index finger over the screen and saw a message from Matt Nava.

This was a surprise. Nava had been one of the cyber experts working under her at Santa Flora PD, back when she'd had the title Detective Lieutenant in front of her name.

He'd sent the message from his personal account with a subject line that read: *What the Hell?*

Opening it, Kate saw a brief paragraph followed by a hyperlink.

Hey Lieutenant,
What the hell's happening here? First Rusty. Now this. Must be something in the water at the safety building. Check it out.
Matt

A glance at the link told her it was from a newspaper in Tallahassee.

For some reason, she felt the small hairs on the back of her neck rise and a nervous flutter form in her gut.

"Rusty" was Rusty Patterson. Her friend and former boss

who had gone from beloved detective to slasher movie psycho, killing an entire family in cold blood.

So *now* what had happened?

She jabbed the link and a news story filled the screen.

The headline read:

MAN TANGLES WITH COPS
CLAIMS HE'S TRACKING "MONSTER"

Next to the story, she saw a picture of someone she knew, and that flutter in her gut turned to stone.

Damn.

2

WHEN KATE SAW JUDGE JOHN HOFFMAN'S mug shot on her cell phone screen, the abrasions on his forehead and cheek drew her gaze first, followed by the purple semi-circle under his eye.

Then she noted how unkempt he looked. His eyebrows and beard were thick tangles of unruly gray and black hair. His hair—once trimmed with precision—now slithered down from his scalp, tendrils of gray hanging just above his shoulders.

Kate had witnessed part of the judge's decline. But at the time, with her own life turned upside down by a bitter divorce and a dying father, she had channeled what little energy she'd had left into her demanding job and paid scant attention to the inevitable gossip.

Now, her gaze shifted from the photo of Hoffman to the

first few paragraphs of the story.

> *By Warner Brown*
> *Staff Writer*
>   *APALACHE SPRINGS, Fla. — A DUI suspect and oust-*
> *ed California judge was jailed last night after a three-mile*
> *chase ended with him allegedly punching a police officer*
> *in the face and claiming he was 'hunting a monster, a*
> *beast.'*
>   *John Hoffman, of Santa Flora, Ca., was booked into jail*
> *on charges of assaulting a police officer, fleeing and*
> *eluding and driving under the influence. Police say the*
> *two patrol officers saw him run through a red light at 8:30*
> *p.m. When they attempted to stop his black Cadillac*
> *sedan, Hoffman sped away, leading police on a chase at*
> *speeds in excess of 100 mph.*
>   *After Hoffman stopped, police say he exited his Cadillac*
> *and approached the two officers. They reportedly ordered*
> *him to stop, but he became more agitated and began*
> *shouting at them.*
>   *"You don't understand. He's a monster! A beast! He'll*
> *kill again!"*
>   *One officer was treated at the scene for minor injuries.*
>   *"The suspect's lucky things ended the way they did,"*
> *said Det. Arlan Miller. "As fast as he was driving, with*
> *his blood alcohol level, he could've killed himself. Or*
> *someone else.*
>   *"Guy acted like he was possessed or something," Miller*
> *said.*

Kate stopped reading, then rested her phone on her thigh and pressed her palms to her eyes, moving them in gentle circles.

She'd known Hoffman for years. They hadn't been all that close, but he'd shown up for her mother's funeral. When she was a senior in high school, her own interest in police work blossoming, she'd landed a summer job in his office.

He'd asked her questions about her mother's case and—she found out later—had more than once harangued the chief about his department's inability to solve the murder. He'd also written a letter of recommendation for her when she'd applied for a job with the department.

All this had come at a time when her father had been too wrapped up in his own pain to do, well, anything at all for Kate.

That had been the *old* Judge John Hoffman.

But then one day his wife and children went on a trip to Florida and had never come back. They'd just disappeared, as though they'd joined the witness protection program. But most people thought his wife had simply pulled off a well-planned escape from their marriage, although they were never quite sure why.

Hoffman's ensuing decline had become the stuff of water cooler legend in law enforcement circles. Some were sympathetic, while others took a certain glee in Hoffman's downfall.

The viciousness hadn't surprised Kate. A judge, especially one with exacting standards and strong opinions, pissed people off. And once Hoffman started hitting the bottle and eventually lost his job? Some saw it as a time to snipe at him without fear of reprisal.

Kate couldn't do it. She'd lost so much in her own life. She had felt for the judge and had privately hoped he'd pull out of his tailspin, a feat he had apparently never managed.

Weston's voice interrupted her thoughts. "You okay?"

She glanced his way, thought she saw concern in his dark

eyes.

"Yes," she said. Even to her own ears, her voice sounded flat, distracted.

"You don't look it."

"I may have a lead."

He looked at her. "On the Harbinger?"

She shook her head. "No, something else."

Holding up her phone, she showed him a blown-up version of Hoffman's picture and recounted the details of the arrest.

His eyes trained on the road, Weston listened in silence, his lips curved into a deep frown. When Kate finished, he waited for a few beats, scratched absently at his scalp.

"That's it? That's all you have?"

"All I have? Just a second ago you were wondering if the Beast was yanking our chain again. What if this is part of it?"

"I was talking about the Harbinger. Some judge gets drunk, talks gibberish and hits a cop, and now you think *that's* the Beast?"

"*Hello…*" Kate said. "You don't think that sounds just like Clyde Stouffer?"

"Stouffer was paling around with the freak. You think a former judge would associate himself with a guy like that? I don't buy it."

She showed him the photo again. "But look at Hoffman's face. Look how far he's fallen. Did you listen to what he said?"

Weston shrugged. "He called someone a monster."

"He called him a beast. And said he was a killer. What makes you so skeptical all of a sudden?"

"Listen," Weston said, "you're talking about a couple of statements reported by the press about a guy pulled over for a drunk driving."

"Right."

"And the statements were taken from a police report. Which was written by a cop."

"Hence the phrase 'police report.'"

"Look at his face," Weston said. "Scrapes and scratches on his forehead. Black eye. Those cops thumped him."

"They probably had no choice. Hoffman was a Marine. Even drunk, he'd still put up a fight."

Weston shook his head. "Even so, those cops gave him a good beating. Probably more than he deserved."

Kate sensed where this discussion was going, an angry heat radiating from her face and neck. "So they piled on, then made up a story about it? Is that what you're saying?"

Weston heaved an exasperated sigh. "Yes, that's what I'm saying. Damn near to the letter."

"Because all cops are liars."

"*Some*," he said. Kate noticed his face had reddened, too. And he held the steering wheel in a two-handed death grip. "Other cops are just stubborn as hell."

Kate frowned. "Oh, how I wish I still had my own goddamned car. This little protest isn't about Hoffman or the Beast at all. It's about you."

"Think about it," he said. "These two cops pull over a drunk. They're hyped from the chase, adrenaline pumping. Then he gets out of the car. He's wasted and all keyed up, so he takes a swing at them. Maybe he pulls some weird moves on them. They lose it and smack him around."

"This is crap..."

"Later, they realize he's not just any drunk, he's a former judge, and he might be connected in ways that could burn them pretty bad. So they make up a story."

"To make him look crazy."

"Yeah."

"Because they want a free pass."

He shrugged again. "Maybe. Tell me it couldn't happen."

"It could happen. But that's not what happened here."

"And you know this because?"

She searched for the words, but came up empty.

"I just know it," she said.

"Because you used to be a cop. And you don't want to believe cops do that."

"I put a cop in jail. For murder. You remember that, don't you? It wasn't that long ago."

"There's nothing there. We should be concentrating on the Harbinger connection, not some old coot with a drinking—"

Stop fighting, please!

The voice sounded in Kate's head, surprising her.

Weston raised his eyes to the rearview mirror and studied Christopher's reflection. He heaved a deep sigh and, when he spoke again, his voice sounded hushed, like a father soothing a child. "Sorry, Chris. We're just having a discussion."

Though still angry, Kate said, "Noah's right. We were just talking."

Your friend. The judge. He wasn't always like this?

Kate shook her head. "He used to be a much different man. Always seemed in control. But then some things happened. And when they did, he fell apart. I've never seen anything like it. It was horrible to watch."

Shifting her position, she looked over the back of her seat at Christopher. His milky white eyes were locked on the window, maybe because it offered at least some contrast between dark and light.

Kate's right. There's something there.

"You mean like with Clyde?" Weston asked. "You think this might be the Beast again?"

I'm not sure. Something. But we shouldn't ignore it.

Still looking doubtful, Weston glanced at Kate, then tightened his grip on the wheel again and punched the accelerator.

3

THE POLICE STATION AND CITY jail were located in a downtown populated by beachwear shops, bars, restaurants and old motels. The stone building housing the station was built to look like a Spanish mission, complete with a roof covered in curved, red tiles.

Weston nosed the Rambler into a parking space in front of the building, turned off the engine and pulled the keys from the ignition. "How much time do you need?"

"You aren't coming?" Kate asked.

"Pass. I don't like police stations. I hate jails even more." He nodded at Christopher in the backseat. "I'm gonna get him some food and some coffee for myself."

He pointed through the windshield at a restaurant located a couple of doors down from the police station. The sign outside read SMITH'S COVE.

"We'll go there," he said. "You can catch up with us when you're done."

Frowning, Kate opened her door. "Fine. I'll see you in a while."

She exited the car and slammed the door. She could already tell Weston was going to make this trip an absolute pain in the ass, at least until he got a real hint of the Beast. He'd told her more than once that Chris doesn't always get it right, and he wasn't yet convinced this was worth their time.

Kate climbed the steps to the lobby, yanked open the door and moved inside. The interior smelled of ammonia and lemon-scented wood polish. A quartet of chairs stood unused, lined up two and two along the walls.

A police officer with thinning brown hair and a matching mustache was seated behind a pane of bulletproof glass, typing something into a laptop. Looking up from the screen, he acknowledged Kate with a nod and turned his focus back to his PC.

"Help you?" he asked.

Acting purely on reflex, Kate almost identified herself as a detective, but caught the words before they came out. During the ride here, she'd worked out a cover story—albeit a thin one—in her head.

"I'm here to see Detective Miller," she said.

"About?"

"Judge John Hoffman."

The officer looked up from his screen and stared at her for several seconds. A toothpick jutted from the corner of his mouth, his lips shaded brown from nicotine. He used his tongue to wag the tip of the toothpick as he studied her for several seconds.

"Hoffman? And you are?"

"Kate Messenger."

"Are you his attorney?"

Kate shook her head.

"Family?"

"No," Kate replied. "I know him... from California."

Kate saw something flicker in the man's eyes and could sense a wall go up. Obviously being a friend of Hoffman's in this town wasn't something she wanted to admit to.

"Actually," she said, "I'm a former colleague of his."

"You're a judge?"

Kate shook her head. "Police officer. Well, former police officer. Santa Flora, California. He was a judge there when I was a cop."

Frowning, the officer leaned forward and narrowed his eyes, scrutinizing her. "You used to be a cop and...?"

Finesse had never been Kate's go-to move. And while she was certainly learning to maneuver her way through this post law enforcement minefield, the violent events in Alabama, coupled with Weston's bad attitude, had stripped her of her patience.

Her expression hardened. She cleared her throat and said, "I'm here because Hoffman got arrested. It's an inquiry."

"An inquiry? Who's inquiring?"

"Santa Flora County. I'm on a contract with them. Not sure how you handle things here, but when a man of his stature goes on a bender in another state, my county takes that shit seriously. Now, do I get to see him or are you gonna fingerprint me and subject me to a cavity search first?"

"Maybe I should call the county."

"Do it," Kate said, "I'm guessing you'll wind up with a shiny new detective's shield for your incredible police work."

"Hey, look—"

"In the meantime, I'm sort of burning daylight here. So if it's not too much trouble, I'd like to speak with Detective Miller."

The cop held up both hands, palms facing Kate. "Easy," he said. "Let me get things moving."

"That would be nice."

The officer reached to his left and picked up a clipboard and slipped it under a small opening beneath the protective glass separating them, along with a pen attached by a thin chain.

"Visitor's log. Sign it and I'll contact Miller."

Kate thanked him and began printing her name on the form while he disappeared into the back of the station.

A couple minutes later, he returned, told her to have a seat in the lobby and went back to working on his laptop.

Eventually, Kate heard the muted beep of someone pushing in a code onto a keypad, followed by the click of a bolt snapping back. She looked up in time to see a steel door leading into the station's interior swinging open. It was accompanied by a loud buzz to alert the other cops and staff that someone was going in or out of the building.

A short, stocky man in brown khakis and a polo shirt ambled into the room. His service pistol was holstered on his right hip and his badge was hooked on the opposite side of the belt's buckle. His shirt's white fabric, straining to contain his thick shoulders and bulging midsection, gleamed under the fluorescent lights.

As he strolled toward her, Kate uncoiled from her chair and gave him a subdued smile.

"I'm Arlan Miller," he said. He nodded his head at the uniformed officer on the other side of the glass. "Bob says you're here to discuss a case of ours. Some kind of county rep?"

"That's correct," she said.

"But you're not a police officer."

"Not anymore," she said, "But I was in the area and I've

been asked by the county to look into this. As you can imagine, they're," Kate paused and looked for the right word, "concerned about his behavior. This all seems a bit out of character for him."

Miller snorted at that. "From what the arresting officers said, he seemed okay with bolting down the freeway at hyper-speed and throwing punches at cops."

Kate felt her stomach clench, but forced a smile. She was here for information, she told herself. Not to rehabilitate Hoffman's damaged reputation.

Miller asked, "So he wasn't like this in California?"

Hesitating, Kate wet her lips with her tongue, looked around the room, as though self conscious and said, "Is there somewhere we can talk?"

4

MILLER USHERED KATE INTO AN interview room. Along the way, they'd stopped in the station's lunchroom and he'd poured each of them a cup of coffee.

The interview room was spartan. White walls and ceiling, nearly white linoleum, the monotony broken by a couple of tattered posters warning against drunk driving and stranger danger. Kate remembered seeing similar posters at her old department before the city had decided to remodel the building.

A rectangular table, ringed by a quartet of folding chairs, stood in the center of the room. He gestured for Kate to take a seat. In one corner, a digital camera stood on a tripod, lens cap in place. A handheld digital recorder, about the size of a candy bar, lay in the middle of the table. Its blank LED screen told Kate it was off.

Setting her coffee on the table top, she eased into one of the chairs. Miller walked halfway around the table, pulled up on his sharply creased pants, and lowered himself into a chair opposite her.

Lacing his fingers together, he set his joined hands on the table top just next to his coffee cup and threw her a warm smile. "What's on your mind, Kate?"

"First," she said. "Is the judge okay?"

Miller's mouth opened, but no sound came out. He blinked. After a long pause, he said, "Frankly, he seems anything but okay. Not that I'm a shrink. If I was, I wouldn't be doing this, right?"

Kate gave him a knowing smile. "You've done it long enough to know you'd rather be doing something else."

He snorted. "I've been a cop for seventeen years. That means eight more until retirement." His mouth turned up at the corners in a playful grin. "I started counting about fifteen years ago."

"Fishing?"

He smiled. "Carpentry. Can't stand seafood. But you didn't come here to discuss my job satisfaction—or lack thereof."

She nodded. "The reason the county called me is because John's a friend of mine. Or he used to be, when I was on the job."

Miller leaned back in his chair, rubbed his chin with his thumb and forefinger, and looked at her. It didn't strike her as an aggressive or condemning stare; just someone watching things unfold.

After more silence, he said, "So, how does a guy like that become a judge in California? I assume he didn't act like this on the bench?"

"No, but John's been... troubled for some time."

Miller nodded. "Again, I'm not a shrink, but I've taken enough psych classes at the local college to know he's paranoid and probably delusional. But that's a layman's view. I'm not walking too far out on a limb here. Most well-adjusted people don't get drunk, lead the police on high-speed chases, or take swings at them, right?"

"No, they don't."

"But this guy did and he's a judge. Or used to be. And you and I have both known some judges with serious issues, but they sure as hell hide it better than Hoffman."

Kate nodded. "He's pretty out there. Are you gonna keep him much longer?"

He shrugged. "It all depends. Since he sobered up, he's acting better. Quieter at least. No more yelling about monsters coming to get him."

"So he hasn't said any more about that?"

"Not a damn thing. The officers at the scene are pretty sure he was trying a little verbal sleight of hand. Make up a crazy story to explain away his even crazier behavior. You know how that works."

"Seen it more times than I want to remember," she said. "But all this talk about someone who'd kill again... Do you think there's anything to it?"

"Do you?"

Kate shrugged. "I don't know what to think when it comes to John."

"Fair enough. Saying he's complicated would be one hell of an understatement. But, look, here's the thing. The judge went on and on about this stuff. How 'they' were going to kill him. How they were coming for him and they wanted to silence him."

"Wait a minute... *they*?"

"They."

She thought about Christopher's friend Lucy, who had been traveling with the Beast, but Christopher had assured them that she knew nothing of the Beast's extracurricular activities. Could this have something to do with the Harbinger? Were they teaming up?

"Did he say who 'they' were?"

"Not a damn word. And when he sobered up, it was like it had never happened."

"He acted normal?"

Miller laughed. "Hell, no. He doesn't have the ability to act normal anymore. I thought we'd established that. But at least he stopped talking about all that crap. All he seemed to care about was getting out of jail. Probably so he could go on another bender." He held up a hand. "No offense."

Kate forced a smile. "None taken."

"You were a cop in his hometown. Does any of his ranting mean anything to you?"

Kate cleared her throat and said, "Nothing comes to mind."

"I didn't think so. Seems to me that if he knew something about a murder, he would have spit out the information while he was drunk. I assume he never came to work in blood-spattered clothes, did he?"

Kate grinned. "Not that I recall."

"Look," Miller said. "There's something bothering me here. I wasn't going to put a lot of energy into it because, frankly, with this being a DUI and a minor assault charge, I didn't think it was worth the effort. But since you're here, let me throw this tidbit out there. Mind?"

Kate shook her head.

Miller pulled a pair of glasses from his shirt pocket and slipped them on. Leaning forward, he flipped open the Hoffman file and leafed through a couple of pages before pausing on a document. The paper was topped by the U.S. Marine Corps seal and midway down Kate could see a brief block of text, too small to read from her vantage point. Miller stared at the sheet for several seconds before shutting the folder and settling back into his chair.

"Says here he's a Marine. Did you know that?"

Kate nodded. "I did."

"You knew he was in Force Recon?"

"Force what?"

"Force Recon. You heard of the Green Berets?"

"Of course."

"Think of Force Recon as the Corps' version of the Berets." He patted the curve of his belly. "I was a jarhead. Not that you could tell now. I tried out for Force Recon and washed out in the first couple of weeks. If he made it through that school, he was a highly trained fighter."

Kate thought she knew where Miller was going and an uneasy feeling crept over her. She kept her expression neutral and said, "I see."

"Look, here's what I'm saying. The judge, at least a couple of decades ago, was an extremely skilled killer. I mean sneak into an enemy barracks at night and slice the throats of every last soldier without ever making a sound kind of killer."

Kate chewed at her lower lip and considered this new information. John had never made a secret of his military service, but he also hadn't shared details about it. At least not with Kate.

"I had no idea," she said.

Miller shrugged. "A lot of those special forces guys don't talk about their service. So if he never said anything, that's not weird. But here's the thing. I've watched the dash cam videos a couple times. When he takes a swing, it's not much to see. He stumbles forward and throws a couple punches."

"He was drunk."

"Sure. Drunk enough to get his ass handed to him by some cops, especially after they pulled out their batons and pepper spray. But so drunk he couldn't fire off one decent punch?" He frowned. "I find that hard to believe."

"So what's your point?"

It was Miller's turn to shrug. "I'm not sure. It just struck me as odd. I thought you might be able to shed some light on why, with his training, he'd wade into a fight, throw two sloppy punches and call it a night."

"I have no clue. Age? Years of drinking? From what I understand, John's life's been one long binge over the last few years. Maybe it's just taken its toll."

"You mean some kind of dementia?"

"Maybe."

"He get in many fights back in California?"

Kate thought about it, wondering if she should have paid closer attention to the gossip. "Not that I remember. Drunk driving, yes. But not fighting. Of course, he knew the local cops pretty well. Maybe he just didn't want to mix it up with them."

Miller gave a non-committal shrug.

"Besides," Kate lied, "if things had been *that* bad, the folks at county would have written him off long ago and they wouldn't have called me." She paused. "You think I could get a copy of the police report?"

Miller shrugged again. "I don't see why not."

"And I'd like to see him."

He spread his hands in a helpless gesture. "I can't do anything about that. He's not here. Once the officers booked him, they transported him to the county jail. And I wouldn't be surprised if they've already scheduled him for arraignment."

Miller glanced at his watch.

"Damn," he said. "I have an interview in a couple of minutes."

He rose from the chair and pulled at the creases in his pant legs to straighten them. Reaching into a pocket, he drew out one of his business cards, tossed it onto the table and focused on gathering up his files.

"Joe up front can make those copies for you," he said without looking up from his papers.

"Are the arresting officers here? I'd like to speak with them, if I could."

"They work midnights. They won't be in for a few hours."

Kate reached into her purse and rummaged around until she found her notepad and pen. She scrawled her name and cell phone number on the paper and set it on the table near Miller.

Picking it up, he glanced at it, then slipped it into his shirt pocket. If her lack of business cards concerned him, he gave no outward signs.

Instead, muttering a hasty goodbye, he shook her hand and led her back to the lobby and told her to wait for the copies.

5

SMITH'S COVE CAFE WAS LONG and narrow, reminding Kate of a double wide trailer as soon as she entered it. The air was tinged with the odor of fried fish, the clanking of silverware against plates and the murmur of a half dozen conversations.

Booths lined one wall and Kate saw Weston seated in the last one, positioning him to watch the door. She barely could see the top of Christopher's head, the back of which was facing her.

Weston paused from slipping a food-laden fork into his mouth and acknowledged her with a two-fingered wave.

She replied with a curt nod, wondering fleetingly why his coolness bothered her, before the sights and smells of food made her realize she was hungry. She strode to the booth and slid in next to Christopher. If her arrival registered with the boy, he didn't show it. A small white plate smeared with apple pie filling and a half-full glass of milk sat in front of him.

Fixing her gaze on Weston, she pointed at Christopher. "Sugar coma or something else?"

"Something else," Weston said. "He's been like this for ten minutes or thereabouts. You get to see your friend?"

She shook her head. "They took him to county lockup. But I don't know if he's still there."

Weston dragged a wadded paper napkin across his mouth and tossed its remains on the table next to his coffee cup. A waitress, a young redheaded woman, took Kate's order before disappearing again to the kitchen.

"Did the cops tell you anything?"

She told him about her subterfuge involving Santa Flora County, then said, "Not that it got me much. The detective I spoke with—"

"Detective? They assigned a detective to a drunk driving rap?"

"I'm thinking it's because the case involves a judge."

"One who says crazy stuff and hits cops."

"You mind if I tell the story?"

"By all means."

"Most of what Miller—that's the detective—said matched the newspaper report. He did say something interesting, though. Apparently, Hoffman was in special forces, which I didn't know."

Weston nodded. "Impressive."

"Miller said this surprised him because he watched the footage of the arrest shot by the cruiser cameras and saw nothing extraordinary about Hoffman's fighting abilities. John took a couple of swings, neither of which did much damage, and the police cuffed and stuffed him."

"He was drunk."

The redheaded waitress glided by the table, placing a cup of coffee in front of Kate before moving on.

"I told Miller the same thing. But he said even drunk John should've put up more of a fight than he did."

"And he bases that belief on…"

"He's a retired Marine. Just like John. And he's familiar with the training."

"That's interesting," Weston said, "but it tells us next to nothing."

Kate ground her teeth together and stared into her coffee. As much as she hated to admit it, he was right. Plus her speculation about the Beast and the Harbinger being the "they" Hoffman had ranted about seemed like a stretch, even to her. Especially since the ranting had stopped as soon as he'd sobered up.

So maybe there was another explanation for his behavior.

Weston said, "Did they find anything interesting in the car?"

Kate shrugged. "I'm not sure yet. I have the incident reports, but not much else."

"Can you get a copy of the video?"

"If I wanted to file a written request, I probably could get it along with a recording of the radio traffic."

"Or you might piss off the local cops just enough that they call Santa Flora to complain."

She nodded. "And the county'll tell them I'm lying and we end up screwed. Good point. I'll scan the Internet later and see whether any of the local TV or radio stations have the footage."

The waitress swung by again, this time setting a slice of apple pie on the table in front of Kate. Kate thanked her. As the woman gathered up some of the empty dishes, Weston asked for the bill. She said she'd be right back with it and left to check on another table.

Kate cut off a mouthful of pie with the edge of her fork, and Weston seemed to sense her preoccupation with what Miller had told her.

"You think this detective has a point?" he asked. "About Hoffman's fighting skills?"

Kate swallowed her pie and cut off another piece with her fork. "It's possible. And it may tell us something."

"Like what?"

"I'm only spitballing here, but if John *was* holding back when he took those swings, then why? He was definitely talking about a monster—more than one, apparently—but what if he was just bullshitting?"

"As in misdirection?"

She nodded. "Detective Miller said Hoffman was trained as a stealth killer. So maybe he was running from something when they pulled him over. Something *he* did. I don't want to believe he's capable of committing any kind of violent crime, but maybe *this* John is."

"So he takes them on a high-speed chase and starts yelling about killers being on the loose when they catch him?" Weston shrugged. "Or maybe I was right in the first place and this is much ado about nothing."

"Maybe. But I don't like the way it feels."

Weston's eyes drifted to the right of Kate. They narrowed and the skin between his eyebrows puckered.

Kate turned and saw Christopher hugging himself and shivering. His eyes were screwed shut, but she could see his eyeballs jerking back and forth beneath the lids, as though he were in the middle of REM sleep. His lips were moving quickly, as though he was doing the impossible and speaking to someone. Yet he was completely silent, not even emitting any grunts or groans.

Kate and Noah exchanged concerned looks. She reached out and touched the boy's arm. He didn't react at all.

Weston said, "Chris?"

Nothing.

"What do you think's happening?" Kate asked.

"Damned if I know."

Kate felt a knot form in her gut. Swallowing hard, she patted the boy's forearm a couple more times, but got no response.

"Is he okay?"

Kate whipped her head toward the voice and saw the waitress standing there, her forehead lined with deep furrows. She was chewing on her lower lip as she watched Christopher.

"I mean, is he having an allergic reaction or something? We try and put allergy warnings on the menu—"

"He's okay," Kate said, forcing what she hoped was a reassuring smile. "We've been traveling for more than a day and he's exhausted."

"He's shivering. I can call a doctor, if you'd like."

"He's fine. We really just need to get him to a motel so he can get a few hours sleep."

Without taking her eyes from Christopher, the woman nodded and set the bill on the table. "I can get that whenever you're ready."

Weston dropped his hand on the check, drew it toward himself and turned it over as he fished in his pants for his wallet.

"I'll cover this," he said. "Why don't you take him to the car?"

Kate slid out of the booth and pulled on Christopher's arm.

He jerked his arm away and a gurgling sound escaped from his mouth as he tried to scream.

6

CHRISTOPHER PULLED HIS ARMS IN close to his chest, crossing them at the wrists and forming a protective "X" over his torso. His lower jaw hung open and a strained croaking noise emanated from his mouth.

"Christopher," Weston said. "It's us, son. Kate and Noah."

The boy gulped air, as though he'd just surfaced after nearly drowning. With a nod, he acknowledged Weston's words. He was squeezing his upper arms with a white-knuckled grip.

Kate reached out to again touch the boy's arm, but checked herself. She had no idea what'd just happened in his mind. The last thing she wanted was to startle him again.

Weston leaned across the table.

"Are you all right?" Weston asked.

The boy nodded once.

Let's go.

"Go where, son?"

Anywhere!

His 'voice' wasn't particularly loud. Yet a sensation like the heated tip of a fireplace poker pierced Kate's forehead and she gasped. A scream welled up inside her, but her throat muscles ensnared the sound, squeezed it until all she could emit was a small croak, just like Christopher.

What the hell?

As her throat opened again, she looked across the table and saw Weston was in similar distress.

An instant later, the pain inside her skull evaporated. Her throat muscles loosened and breathing grew easy again. She gulped in a deep breath and the black spots that'd been swimming in her vision dissolved.

Kate opened her mouth to speak, but Weston gestured for her to stay quiet. He grabbed the check, motioned toward the door and said, "Go."

Kate became aware of the people at neighboring tables staring at them. Nodding her agreement, she slid out of the booth.

•

It took Kate a couple of minutes to lead Christopher out of the diner and onto the sidewalk. Even in the late afternoon, the sun was hot, and she guided him underneath the awning poised over the diner's front window. He was again hugging himself, tears streamed down his face.

I'm sorry.

"It's okay. Forget it," Kate said. "Just tell me what happened."

I don't know.

"Do you remember anything?"

He stood motionless for a minute. Kate assumed he was

trying to search his memory for a reason for his behavior.

I finished eating. Noah asked if I wanted anything else. I told him no. Next thing I knew, it was like I'd come back from somewhere, but I couldn't breathe. I was terrified.

"What were you scared of?"

I don't know.

"How could you not know?"

I don't remember. Everything went black. I didn't faint. It was like someone flipped a switch. Nothing. Then they flipped the switch again and I was awake. Terrified.

Kate felt a nervous flutter in her stomach. In the short time she'd known him, she'd certainly seen him upset, but most of the time he'd appeared unflappable, unscathed by events —including getting his tongue cut out by a madman—that would've sent most adults scrambling for a shrink's couch.

Had they missed something? Was he starting to break down under the strain of everything he'd experienced? He was, after all, just a boy.

God help her, had Kate been a party to it? She was traversing the country, partnered with a difficult and damaged man with no law enforcement experience.

And a child.

Hunting a murderous psychopath who knew they were on his trail.

Even as the enormity of that settled on her again, she felt someone by her side. She turned and saw Weston at her elbow. Judging by the sour look on his face, he'd been privy to Christopher's thoughts, too.

Chris," he said, "what do you remember? Anything at all?"

The boy shook his head, then released his arms and let his hands hang at his sides. His posture changed, his spine growing erect. He stuck out his chest. For reasons she couldn't explain, the change sent a cold stab of fear shooting up her spine. It was as though someone—or something—else controlled him.

Whatever had happened, he no longer looked like a scared child.

I'm okay.

"Good," Noah said, but didn't sound convinced. He turned and looked in Kate's direction. "The waitress suggested a motel just down the road from here. We should go ahead and grab a room before it gets any later. This place doesn't seem like a tourist mecca, but we may as well make sure we have a place to sleep."

•

Weston parked the Rambler in the lot outside the motel, a dump called the Jolly Roger Inn. Kate stayed in the car with Christopher.

The boy sat motionless in the backseat. Kate tried to draw him out a couple of times by asking him questions. When she got no reply, she decided to focus on finding Hoffman.

She accessed the Internet through her phone and scoured around until she found the Court Clerk's website. She punched in Hoffman's name and found his arraignment had been scheduled to start a little less than an hour earlier.

Shit.

Going to the arraignment would've been the easiest way to meet up with him face to face and that wasn't likely to happen now.

Then again, court didn't always start on time and maybe they could catch the tail end of the proceedings.

Weston exited the motel office and made his way to the car. Climbing inside, he handed Kate a key card.

"We should unpack," he said.

"Not yet," she told him. "If we hurry, and the afternoon

calendar's full, we could still make it to John's arraignment. He may not have been called yet."

"The boy needs rest."

Kate could feel frustration well up inside her. She wanted to look for Hoffman, but she also knew Weston was right. She had found Christopher's behavior at the restaurant as unnerving as he did, maybe more so.

In spite of the boy's amazing abilities, and the fact that he himself had initiated this quest, Kate at times struggled with what they were doing. In her former life, if she'd found two other adults doing the same thing, she would've arrested them and fought like hell to get the kid to safety.

Yet here she was.

What a difference a few weeks had made.

When she'd first met these two, it had been at a murder scene. She'd dropped in after work, compelled by what she'd thought at the time was simply her gut.

She later found out that Christopher had used his mental abilities to prod her into visiting the crime scene. What had seemed like an act of freewill, a detective following her instincts, later turned out to have its roots in mental manipulation.

At times like this, when she thought about the risks they were taking, she began to wonder all over again: Was this really a good idea? Or was she being manipulated somehow?

A mental hall of mirrors.

Kate said, "You're right. Why don't we take him to the room and give him some down time while you and I check out the arraignment."

"This guy is *your* friend. What do you need me for?"

"Look, I know you think this is a wild goose chase, but Chris said we should check into it, so that's what we're gonna do. Both of us."

"After what he just went through? I don't think he should be left—"

It's okay, Noah, Chris suddenly said, back again from wherever he'd gone. *I'll be okay by myself. Kate's right. You need to go, too.*

"Are you sure?" Weston asked.

I'm sure.

7

WHEN THEY REACHED THE COURTHOUSE, Weston spun
the Rambler around the block in search of a parking space,
but couldn't find one. Kate checked her watch and bit off a
curse.

Just ahead, a blue U.S. mail box stood next to the curb.
Kate pointed at it. "Drop me there, and catch up to me after
you've parked."

Weston guided the Rambler up to the curb and she exited,
stepped onto the sidewalk, and hurried through a courtyard.
It was late afternoon and still hot.

A revolving door flanked on either side by glass doors led
into the courthouse.

She noticed a pair of women standing next to one of the
doors. One smoked a cigarette and nodded with metronome-
like steadiness, listening as the other gestured wildly, grous-

ing about the various misdeeds of someone named Daryl. As Kate moved closer to them, she got the impression Daryl's bad behavior was a frequent topic of discussion.

The only other person in the courtyard was a tall, lanky man with a shaved head, wearing jeans and an avocado-colored polo shirt. He was seated on the lip of a large water fountain, an unlit cigarette sticking out from his mouth. His eyes were covered by mirrored sunglasses, but his face was turned in Kate's direction.

She sensed his gaze on her and it made the small hairs on the back of her neck stand up, sparking a primal urge to run, like an antelope sensing a lion.

What the hell?

Kate was many things, some damn unpleasant.

A delicate damsel she was not.

Maybe it was the byproduct of growing up with an emotionally distant father. Maybe it came from having her mother murdered when she was just a teen.

Whatever. She wasn't much for grabbing her pearls and shrieking.

When Mr. Sunglasses realized she saw him, he turned his head and made a show of searching his pants pockets for something.

Kate's gut told her he was bad news.

But should that surprise her? She was at a courthouse.

Hurrying past the two women, she pushed through the revolving doors and into the courthouse lobby.

She'd left her purse and her gun in the Rambler. Since she couldn't legally carry a firearm on her person anymore, she didn't want it accessible to Chris or anyone else who might get curious about it. So after her SUV was torched, she'd started storing it in the Rambler's spare tire well and planned to buy a lockbox for added protection.

When she reached the walk-through metal detectors, she set her wallet and her watch in a rectangular plastic basket and loaded it onto a short conveyor belt that would carry it through a screening device.

A male deputy with a ruddy complexion, his gray hair trimmed into a crew cut, gestured without enthusiasm for her to pass through a metal detector. In the meantime, a female deputy kept her eyes fixed on a monitor displaying the insides of Kate's wallet as it passed through the scanner.

According to the Court Clerk's website, Hoffman was supposed to appear before a Judge Jason Ortega. Though she assumed she'd missed the proceedings, Kate hoped she might find Hoffman lingering near the courtroom.

It was a thin hope, but worth a try.

As she collected her things, Kate asked the male deputy for directions to Ortega's court.

"The drunk judge?" He looked at his watch. "Must be your lucky day. They got a late start. Hearing room four. Second floor. You with the press?"

Kate shook her head. "Why do you ask?"

"Got a few reporters up there," he said. "Must be a slow news day."

Damn, she thought. Had she walked into the middle of a media circus? That definitely was not what she needed today.

She rode the elevator to the second floor, stepped out and looked around for the courtrooms, and to her surprise, heard someone to her left shout, "Katie Messenger!"

The voice struck a chord with her, one that caused her stomach to plummet.

Shifting her gaze to the left, she spotted a middle-aged woman standing at the other end of the corridor, waving her arms. Grinning, the woman broke away from the knot of people clustered around her and marched toward Kate.

Kate's expression went stony, and she cocked her fists on her hips and acknowledged the other woman with a faint nod. "Hello, Cindy."

Cindy Davis had been a criminal justice reporter for the Los Angeles Times until she'd lost her job in a round of layoffs. Kate didn't make it a habit to wish bad things on others, but she hadn't been particularly devastated to hear Davis had been shown the door.

Five years earlier, Davis had written a series of stories about cold cases, most of them in California. The series included a piece about the murder of Kate's mother, Cassandra.

Before she wrote the story, Davis had asked Kate multiple times for interviews. And after Kate had refused, Davis complained to Kate's supervisor, Rusty Patterson.

The ultimate media whore, Patterson had pressured Kate into agreeing to the interview.

"Just do it," he'd said. "Maybe someone who knows something will see the story and send us a tip. Break the whole damn thing open. Wouldn't that be great?"

Kate couldn't argue with his logic—or his rank. She'd held her nose and agreed to the interview, which, in and of itself, turned out to be painless.

But Davis had interviewed someone who had said Cassandra had been involved in an affair and her murder was the work of a jilted lover. The same individual, under the cloak of anonymity, had said Kate's father was bad tempered and capable of beating someone to death.

Kate never had identified the source. Though she'd known better than to believe those lies, they had devastated her late father. It was one of the few times in her life she'd actually felt sorry for him.

To Kate's mind, Davis losing her job had been a karmic

kick in the teeth. But Cindy took one of the stories from her series, expanded it into a true crime book and wound up with a bestseller. The last Kate had heard, she'd sold the movie rights for a tidy sum and was on the hunt for a new project.

So much for karma.

In a phone call after the cold case story appeared, Kate had given Davis a royal ass chewing. She'd suggested that Cindy steer clear of Santa Flora and Kate—forever—and Davis had been smart enough to oblige.

Kate had later seen her interviewed on television and the Internet, hawking her true crime book, and the physical change had been striking. Davis had traded in jeans, T-shirts, and sensible shoes for tailored power suits accented by expensive pumps and pearls. The reporter's straight, mouse-brown hair now was dyed honey blonde and adorned with expertly applied highlights and cascaded in waves well past her shoulders.

From what Kate had heard, Davis's publisher had hired an image coach to make her more appealing to television audiences.

Coral snakes are pretty, too, Kate thought. Until they bite you.

Davis bustled up to Kate, got in her space and touched her arm. "Katie, what are you doing here?"

She'd never let anyone but her ex-husband call her that.

"Kate," she said.

"What?"

"My name is Kate. But I know details aren't your specialty."

Davis drew back her hand as though it had been scorched, crossed her arms over her chest. Taking a step back, she pursed her lips and studied Kate over the rims of her eyeglasses.

"You're still mad, aren't you?"

Kate bit down on an angry reply. She didn't have time for this. "Why are you here?"

"Research," Davis said.

"On Judge Hoffman?"

Davis nodded over her shoulder at the courtroom. "That old drunk? No, of course not. I'm working on a new book."

Kate didn't believe this for a nanosecond. "Uh-huh."

"It's a follow-up. Another unsolved murder."

"Last I checked," Kate said, "the judge is still alive. Or are you gonna quote someone anonymously saying he's dead?"

Davis's eyes narrowed. When she spoke again, Kate detected an edge in her voice. "My God, you're an angry woman. It's no wonder you got fired."

"Fired? I didn't get fired."

Davis smirked and cocked an eyebrow. "That's not the way Bob MacLean tells it."

Of course it isn't, Kate thought.

She and MacLean had always had a volatile rivalry, so it didn't surprise her that he'd spin her sudden departure from the department in a way that best suited him.

Wanting to refute this ridiculous slice of nonsense, she started to speak, but felt a hand rest on her shoulder. She wheeled around, ready to smack it away, when she realized it was Weston's. With everything else going on, she'd forgotten all about him.

"Everything all right?" he asked. He gestured at Davis with his chin.

Kate nodded. "Fine," she said. "Let's go."

Her steps quickened by anger, she strode toward the courtroom. She was clenching her teeth so hard, her jaw was starting to ache.

"Who was that?" Weston asked.

"A reporter."

"She famous? I swear I've seen her before."

Kate was about to reply, but stopped short when the double doors leading into the courtroom fanned open and Hoffman came through them, shadowed by a young woman dressed in a black pinstripe suit, a briefcase clutched in one hand.

Behind them towered a grim-faced man, his face tanned, his white hair neatly trimmed over his ears and combed back from his forehead, exposing a sharp widow's peak. His nose curved, telling Kate it had been broken at least once. Small brown eyes scanned the room slowly as he kept pace with Hoffman and the woman.

Judging by the way he carried himself—confident and aware—Kate guessed that, like Hoffman himself, he was former military. And whatever skills he'd gained as a soldier were still available to him when needed.

Kate halted so suddenly that Weston bumped into her shoulder.

He cursed under his breath.

Kate couldn't hear the words and she didn't care. She'd switched her focus to Hoffman, who she only vaguely recognized, even after seeing the news photo. He clutched a battered black satchel under one arm, and his once meticulously cut hair was now long and white, pulled into a ponytail. His beard and mustache were thick and unkempt, hiding his lips. His shoulders appeared stooped. Kate couldn't tell whether it was from frailty or some kind of emotional weight.

His feet, shod in scuffed black wingtips, shuffled slowly over the carpet and his eyes were trained on the floor. He wore a dark-blue suit and a necktie that hadn't been in style for at least a decade.

"That's your friend?" Weston asked.

Kate nodded, but said nothing.

The small group of reporters descended on Hoffman. A petite redhead flanked by a burly cameraman stepped into Hoffman's path, pushed a microphone into his face and blurted out her name and news affiliation. Before she could utter her question, Hoffman batted the microphone from his face and pushed past her.

Kate watched as Hoffman's attorney grabbed his arm, leaned in and whispered something in his ear. The attorney spun around, stepped between Hoffman and the small knot of journalists and began speaking to the reporters. The man who looked former military stood behind, glowering at everyone, while Hoffman broke away and trudged toward the elevators.

Kate stood against the wall and let him pass by. He hadn't yet noticed her and she wanted him away from the reporters and his attorney before she'd approach.

Just as Hoffman reached the elevators, Cindy Davis appeared at his side. She put one hand on his shoulder and with a finger from the other hand jabbed the "down" button. Hoffman whipped his head toward the reporter. Kate tensed. She wasn't sure how he'd react to a stranger stepping into his path again.

Hoffman jerked his arm away and muttered something. Kate couldn't hear the words, but the menacing tone was audible. Davis paled, drew back her hand, and nodded. Any other time, Kate might have enjoyed seeing Davis get slapped down. Right now she was more focused on making sure Hoffman didn't do anything stupid.

The elevator doors parted. Hoffman lurched forward and slipped inside. Davis, her initial surprise gone, took a step forward to follow him, but Weston moved into her path, allowing Kate to follow instead.

As the doors slid closed, Hoffman turned toward Kate and squinted at her.

She flashed him a tight smile. "Hello, John."

8

THE OLD MAN TENSED. EYES narrowed, brow furrowed, he studied Kate as the elevator car began to drop, clutching the battered satchel to his chest now, as if he were afraid she might snatch it. But when they reached the first floor, his expression softened and she saw a trace of recognition in his eyes.

"Kate?"

She nodded. "It's good to see you."

"What the hell are you doing here?"

"I came because of you."

The elevator door opened. She turned and moved into the lobby, with Hoffman just behind her, patting his pockets and mumbling to himself. He looked up, noticed Kate watching him and said, "Sunglasses. Eyes aren't worth shit in this sun. Too old. Too damn old. Did the department send you?"

She shook her head. "I'm not with the department any-more."

"Oh, I hadn't heard. How does your father feel about that?"

"I don't think he gives a damn. He's dead. But then he rarely approved of anything I did while he was alive."

Hoffman stopped fishing through his pockets and turned his eyes up until they met hers. "I'm sorry to hear that, Kate. Mitch was... an interesting man."

Despite herself, Kate felt a small ache forming in her throat and swallowed hard to clear it. She'd tried to think as little as possible about her father. His death had saddled her with a lot of conflicting emotions, most of which she had no interest in feeling.

"Look, John, we don't have much time. What happened with the traffic stop?"

He ducked his head and continued frisking himself for his sunglasses. "I had too much to drink."

"Yeah, I sort of figured that out. You blew a pretty high number."

"If you're here for an intervention, you're too late."

Kate frowned. "Why did you take a swing at those cops?"

"Like I said, I was drunk."

"Bullshit."

His head jerked up and he glared at her.

Kate tensed. Her mouth went dry and she felt her pulse quicken. She didn't expect Hoffman to turn violent, but he'd shown how unpredictable he could be. She kept her eyes locked on his.

"John, I've come a long way—"

"Nobody asked you to."

"You're right. But I did and, well, here the fuck I am." She cast a look to her right, then her left. "I don't see anyone else here for you. Your family's not here."

His glare intensified. "That was out of line."

Kate jabbed a finger at him. "Look, John, you were talking about monsters, people getting killed. You went on a high-speed chase. You assaulted a police officer. But now it's like nothing ever happened. What the hell is going on?"

"It's not your problem. I came here to fix something."

"Good job."

He waved dismissively. "You always did have a smart..." He stopped himself as his gaze focused over Kate's shoulder.

In her periphery, she saw someone approaching. She turned and spotted the judge's attorney and her white-haired partner emerge from the elevator, both glaring, marching toward her. Weston was a couple of paces behind them.

"Excuse me!" the woman called from across the lobby.

Kate ignored her and turned back to Hoffman. "I want an explanation, John. You can at least give me that much."

He softened slightly. "It involves my children. But that's all I can say right now." He gestured toward his attorney. "Look, I have to speak with her. Contact me in twenty minutes."

"Where?"

He gave her the name of a motel and his room number.

As he uttered the last words, the woman stepped between them. "Excuse me," she said. "I'm Angela Lowenthal, Judge Hoffman's attorney. Are you with the media?"

Kate forced herself to take a step back and shook her head. "I'm an old friend of the judge's family. I just wanted to say hi."

Lowenthal nodded, her lips twisting into a cross between a smirk and a smile. "What a wonderful coincidence. You being in town and all. Anyway, I need to speak with my client before it gets any later. You'll have to excuse us."

Before Kate could reply, Lowenthal took hold of Hoffman's upper arm and led him away. To Kate's surprise, he didn't resist. He slipped on his sunglasses and followed her out the door.

Kate was staring after them as Weston appeared next to her.

"What was that all about?"

"Just an attorney protecting her client," Kate said.

"Maybe."

Kate heard the doubt in Weston's voice, but didn't press him on it. He was probably on the verge of telling her—yet again—how they were wasting their time. And she was on the verge of telling him to stick it.

Weston heaved a sigh. "I need to talk to you about something."

"Just save me the grief, okay? I already know you—"

"No," he said. "It's something that reporter told me."

Kate frowned. "Oh, wonderful. What?"

Weston looked around, let his eyes linger on the two deputies at the security station before fixing his gaze on her.

"Not here," he said.

9

KATE COULDN'T QUITE BELIEVE HER ears.

"Are you kidding me? Because if this is a joke, it isn't funny."

They were outside the courthouse now, nearing the Rambler. Weston held up his hands. "I'm just passing along what she told me."

"So Cindy Davis thinks Hoffman is the Harbinger."

"She said one of her sources told her that, but she isn't sure what to believe. That's why she was at Hoffman's hearing today."

"I know this woman, Noah. You can't trust her. She makes things up."

"She told me you'd say that." Turning, he pulled out his keys and walked around the front of the Rambler to the driver's side door.

"At least she got one fact right," Kate said. "Did she have anything else to say about me? Or Hoffman, for that matter?"

"Nothing about you."

"Then what else did she tell you?"

"Not much. But if she's wondering about Hoffman, maybe we should be, too."

Unlocking the car, he pulled open the door, folded into his seat, slid the key into the ignition and looked at Kate as she just stood there trying to process all of this.

Reaching across the seat, Weston cracked open her door.

"Bus is leaving," he said. He turned his eyes ahead, twisted the key, and the engine rumbled to life.

Kate opened her door and got inside. "So what are you thinking? That he's another Clyde?"

"I'm not ready to go that far."

"Then what *are* you saying?"

"Just to keep your eyes open. That's all. Did he tell you anything worth hearing?"

Kate shook her head and pulled her door closed. "No. He mentioned his kids and bitched about getting old."

"You ask him about his run-in with the police?"

"I asked the questions. He dodged them. If I'd had time, I probably could've gotten more information from him, but his lawyer stepped in and shut us down."

"Yeah, she was a princess. But she didn't strike me as a public defender, and Hoffman looks pretty damned destitute. So, how can he afford her?"

Kate shrugged. "I have no idea. Maybe she's working pro bono, or she's a friend of his."

"Assuming he has any left," Weston said, then sighed. "So what's next?"

"We'll find out in about fifteen minutes."

"What do you mean?"

"John wants to meet with me."

"Meet with you? Are you serious?"

"As a heart attack," she said.

•

Hoffman's motel was a pair of red brick, single-story buildings, standing side by side. All the doors were painted orange. Years of exposure to the Florida sun had left the paint faded and blistered. Weather beaten sheets of plywood, marred by graffiti, covered some of the windows.

"Lovely," Weston said. "This just gets better and better."

Kate ignored him. She swept her eyes over the parking lot, scanning it for Hoffman's vehicle. The article had said he was driving a black Cadillac sedan at the time of his arrest. The only black car she saw was a late model Pontiac, right rear tire flat. A white compact car and a large pickup truck were also parked in front of the building.

Weston guided the Rambler through the lot. As it crept along, Kate noted all three vehicles carried Florida license tags. None were vanity plates. The registration sticker on the Pontiac was a different color than that of the other vehicles. She guessed it had expired. Maybe the car belonged to a longtime resident or the motel's owner.

Kate was only vaguely aware of her mind gathering and sifting through these details. After years as a street cop and detective, her brain just went there.

A slim man decked out in an unbuttoned Hawaiian shirt, shorts, and flip-flops, sat on a lawn chair outside one of the rooms. The door next to him stood open. Kate could hear rock music blaring from inside.

Raising a can of beer to his lips, he kept his eyes fixed on the Rambler as it rolled by.

"I'm gonna park," Weston said.

Kate shook her head. "Let's check out the rest of the property first."

"You're the boss."

Kate stiffened. There was a tone to Weston's voice that annoyed her. As if he were merely tolerating her.

He and Christopher had been hunting the Beast for nearly a year before she met them, and despite these last few weeks together—and all that had gone down in Alabama—she knew he still viewed her as an outsider, an interloper. He only put up with her presence in their lives because Christopher wanted her here.

What she'd learned in those weeks, however, was that Weston was smart, focused, and gutsy. He'd been a successful businessman, so he knew how to lead and wasn't all that interested in taking direction. But Kate was a trained and seasoned investigator, and whether he liked it or not, she was going to speak her mind in the field.

Weston drove around to the second of the two buildings. A maroon-colored Lexus SUV, an older model Honda, and a gray Ford sedan were parked there.

Kate glanced at him and saw he was studying the cars, too.

"Nice wheels," he said.

"Judging by the surroundings, it's probably a john hooking up with a prostitute. Or maybe it's a couple of coworkers doing a little team-building exercise."

Weston pointed at the Ford. "That's a cop car if I ever saw one."

Kate nodded, figuring he was right. When they drove past it, she noted that it had black and white U.S. government plates.

"Not surprising," she said. "But that doesn't mean it's got anything to do with Hoffman. A place like this? There are a million reasons they could be here."

"You're the professional."

There was that tone again. She whipped her head around and glared at him. "If you have something to say, spit it out."

Weston hit the brake and the Rambler jerked to a stop.

"Look," he said. "I'm sorry your friend's life took a wrong turn. Truly sorry. And I'm really trying to get on board here, but the more I think about it, the more ridiculous this seems. I let that reporter sway me for a minute, thinking there might be more to this guy, but if he's lucid enough to be setting up meetings with you, he's obviously no Clyde, and I *really* doubt he's the Harbinger."

He gestured to the motel.

"I mean, look at this place. Does this guy have a problem? You bet. But the only thing he has in common with that shit-kicker in Alabama is the bottle. And that's *his* problem. Not ours. Everything else is nonsense."

"You don't know that for sure."

"The hell I don't. I saw the guy. And I know when a man's given up. *I* was that man, not that long ago."

"Yet look at you now."

Weston frowned. "Face it—Hoffman's done and that reporter friend of yours is chasing ghosts. You want to know why he told you to meet him here?"

"Illuminate me," Kate said.

"Because the only thing a guy who's given up loves more than booze is an audience. So he can tell the world about the raw deal he got. We're wasting precious time when we could be doing more productive things."

"Are you forgetting about Christopher? He said we need to explore this."

"Maybe he's only saying that because he knows how you feel about this guy." Weston sighed. "But screw it. We're

66

here now. I'll listen to what Hoffman has to say, but if I don't like what I'm hearing, we forget about him and start focusing on why we came to Florida in the first place. If the Harbinger has a connection to the Beast, he needs to be our first priority."

He turned away from her and hit the gas, wheeling the Rambler around to the front of the motel, where he slid into a parking space.

Grabbing the handle, Kate popped open the door and set a foot on the asphalt. "You are *such* an asshole sometimes."

Before Weston could reply, she'd climbed out and slammed the door behind her. Cocking her hands on her hips, she swept her eyes over the motel grounds.

The guy with the beer was gone, his door shut and the music turned down. If she were still wearing a badge and a gun, she would've guessed he'd made her as a police officer.

She looked toward the door with the room number Hoffman had given her, but his Cadillac was still nowhere nearby. She checked her watch and saw they were on time.

So was Weston right?

Instinct had told her to follow this lead, and Christopher had agreed.

But had they both been wrong?

She pushed her doubts aside and headed for Hoffman's room, hearing Weston's car door open behind her. The best thing she could do was talk to Hoffman, see if he'd offer her more than some cryptic rambling about fixing something to do with his kids.

Weston caught up to her and when they reached the door, Kate rapped her knuckles against it. Weston stood to one side, arms crossed over his chest, expression neutral.

Several seconds passed without a response. Kate strained her ears, listening for signs that Hoffman was inside. A television's soft murmur. Footsteps. Bed springs squeaking as he shot to his feet.

Nothing.

Damn it.

She knocked again and got more of the same.

She glanced at Weston, expecting to see a triumphant look etched on his handsome features, but his face betrayed nothing.

Instead, he gave a small shrug. "Maybe he's still getting his car out of hock."

"Maybe," Kate said. "I guess we should go."

Weston was about to reply when his eyes drifted past Kate and his brow furrowed.

"What?"she asked, then wheeled around in time to see a blonde woman in a black business suit exiting the motel office. Though her eyes were covered by mirrored sunglasses, the woman obviously was scrutinizing them as she marched in their direction.

When she got within several feet, she flipped open a black leather wallet, lifted it so they could see its contents—a badge and ID card all too familiar to Kate.

"FBI," the woman said. "Agent Lara Page. I'd like to speak with you."

10

AGENT PAGE LED THEM INSIDE the motel office.

A young man in a gray suit stood in one corner, arms crossed over his chest. His eyes settled on Kate, lingering long enough to piss her off, and all but ignored Weston.

Page jerked a thumb at the door.

"Watch for Hoffman," she said.

The guy nodded.

Page walked them around the motel's front desk and into a small room. A folding card table topped by a coffee maker, foam cups, and packets of sugar and cream, stood against one wall. A half-eaten glazed donut rested on a paper napkin next to a short stack of folders.

Two folding chairs were pushed under the table. Page gestured at them. "Maybe you two should sit."

"I'll stand," Kate said.

Weston stayed put and said nothing.

Nodding, Page plucked her sunglasses off, folded them, set them on the table and studied Kate and Weston. "Okay, suit yourselves. I just thought it might make things easier."

Silence fell over the room. Kate kept her expression stony, but a nervous flutter disturbed her stomach.

What had they walked into?

"IDs on the table," Page said. "Now."

Kate slipped her California driver's license from her jeans and tossed it onto the table. Page leaned forward, glanced at it, then turned her attention to Weston. He'd taken his wallet from his back pocket, opened it and slid his driver's license from a plastic sleeve. He started to toss it onto the table, but checked himself. "Are we under arrest?"

"What do you think?"

"I think that's not an answer."

"All right," Page said. "No, you and Ms. Messenger aren't under arrest. You're here for a friendly talk. Another minute of your horseshit, though, and that could change."

Kate clenched her jaw. She knew from personal experience that Weston's defensiveness around cops could trigger innate suspicions.

He tossed his driver's license on the table.

Page scanned it and said, "Are you two friends of the judge?"

"More like professional acquaintances," Kate told her. "I was a detective in Santa Flora."

"A detective?"

"A lieutenant. Major Crimes division."

"So, you knew him professionally?"

"Yes."

"Were you traveling with him?"

Kate shook her head. "No."

"Have you ever traveled with him?"

"No."

"You just happened to be in Florida. On the other side of the country from where you work as a detective."

"Worked. Past tense."

"So you're not a police officer anymore."

"No."

"Why not?"

"I resigned."

"Interesting."

"Not really," Weston said. "Unless you're looking for a reason to harass someone. Then it's probably interesting as hell."

Page glared at him. "I take it you *weren't* a police officer?"

Weston snorted. "No, ma'am."

"Did I say something funny?"

"Not yet," he told her.

"Back to my questions. You two just happened to be in Florida at the same time as the judge?"

"A lot of people come to Florida," Weston said. "It's called tourism."

Page let her eyes roll down Weston, who was dressed in jeans and a black T-shirt. "You're a tourist? Are you wearing that to the beach?"

"Did I *say* I was a tourist?"

Her eyes locked on him, Page's jaw clenched and she pursed her lips.

"We'll come back to that," she said. "But you were in Florida and you saw Judge Hoffman in the news."

"Something like that."

"Just something? Or exactly like that?"

"Is John in trouble?" Kate asked.

Page flashed a tight smile and gestured to the chairs.

"Why don't you two sit down? Really. I need to go make a couple of phone calls."

11

KATE AND WESTON SAT IN the cramped room, drank coffee, and waited for Agent Page to return.

With her phone, Kate accessed her email and checked her
voice messages. As she dialed through the prompts, a part of
her was hoping to find a message from Hoffman.

Instead, she found an automated call alerting her to a
recall on an SUV that was nothing more than a burnt out
shell she'd left behind in Alabama.

Oh, how she missed that car.

She deleted that message and listened to the second one.
No one spoke. But for several seconds, she heard cars
whooshing by and a horn honking in the background. Then
the line went dead. Checking the envelope information, she
found the call had come ten minutes ago from an unidenti-
fied number.

Could it have been Hoffman? Possibly.

She'd had the same cell number for years.

Setting her phone on the table, she filled a foam cup three quarters of the way with coffee, offered some to Weston who waved her off. Just as she placed the carafe back into the coffee maker, Agent Page entered the room, followed by her partner.

Page leaned against a wall and crossed her arms over her chest.

"We did some checking," she said. "Found all kinds of interesting things." She nodded to Weston. "Particularly about you. Quite a background you have there."

Weston's face remained impassive. Kate knew what Page was driving at. If they'd gotten a hint about the murder of his family, it would surely pique their interest.

Page shifted her gaze to Kate. "And you, Ms. Messenger, how did you go from a major crimes detective to best buddies with a pair murder suspects? How exactly does that happen? Are you some kind of groupie?"

"She traded up," Weston said.

Kate ignored him. "*Pair* of suspects? What the hell does that mean?"

She saw something flicker in the other woman's eyes.

"You know Mr. Weston's a suspect in a murder in North Carolina, correct?"

She nodded. "I also know the district attorney never made the charges stick against him. The forensics didn't match. He had a solid alibi. I questioned him about it when I was with the Santa Flora police department."

"You must've liked what you heard," Page said.

"'Liked' isn't the word I'd use."

"And what about Hoffman?"

"The judge? What about him?"

Page cocked an eyebrow. "You like the bad boys, don't you?"

Messenger frowned and turned her gaze on Page's partner. "Does your young protégé ever speak, or does he just stand there trying to look intimidating?"

Neither agent said anything, letting time stretch a little. Kate knew the technique. Let the uncomfortable silence build until it envelops the room, and hope your suspect gets antsy enough to spit out something stupid.

Kate crossed her legs and forced a smile. She knew the game, but she wasn't playing. Instead, she focused on the air conditioner humming in the window. Weston's hands were resting in his lap, left on top of right, and he stared down at them. Kate knew from her own experience with him in the hot seat that he was as well-versed at this game as she was.

"If you have a point to make," he said to Page, "maybe you ought to make it."

"All right," she said.

She opened the folder she was carrying, leafed through its contents until she found what she was looking for. Pulling a couple of photos from it, she then stepped forward and tossed them on the table.

"Take a look," she said.

Kate picked one up, looked it over and felt her stomach roll.

The photo was of a woman. Or, more specifically, a female torso, pale and bloodless, positioned on a plastic sheet. In the upper left corner of the frame lay the woman's head. Long tendrils of dark hair stretched out over the plastic. The flesh was discolored and puffy. Dark smears of mud slashed across the abdomen and shoulders.

"Does she have a name?" Kate asked.

"Probably," the male agent said. "Damned if we know it,

though."

Kate nodded. She glanced at Weston, who was looking at another photo.

Page gestured to him. "The one your boyfriend's looking at—"

"He's not my boyfriend."

"Her name's Anna Carroll. Cops found her in a ditch a few months ago, along a stretch of interstate in Georgia. From what we've gathered, she was hooking at a truck stop in Jacksonville. She hung around there for a while, then disappeared. That was six months ago."

Weston slid the photo across the table to Kate, who snatched it up. Another torso set out on a plastic sheet, this time with the head still connected. Judging by the skin color, Kate guessed the woman was dead for quite some time before her body was located.

"A dog found this one. Guy was walking him in the woods. Some neighborhood filled with McMansions in the Atlanta suburbs. The dog bolts off, runs into a culvert and won't come back. The owner thinks this is weird. He hunts down the dog and finds it with Ms. Carroll's body."

Kate handed the photos back to Page. The agent took them and slipped them back into her folder, closed it and tucked it under her arm.

"We've linked at least three other victims to this case," she said. "All women. All hookers from Florida. All dismembered, the bodies dumped in other states. Just the torsos."

"To make them harder to identify," Kate said.

Page nodded. "In Ms. Carroll's case, we think her body was partially intact because the killer was rushed in some way. We were able to use dental records to identify her. We also found a pair of shorts nearby. Denim cutoffs, like the ones witnesses said she was wearing when she went missing. We found the heads in two other cases, which helped us ID the vics."

Weston leaned back in his chair, raised his hands, laced the fingers and brought them behind his head. He cut loose with an exasperated sigh.

"Fascinating stuff," he said. "But I have no idea how it relates to us. I can guarantee I haven't been to this state in over a year, and I've enough evidence in my dash to prove it."

The last time he'd been to Florida, Kate thought, would've been to pick up Christopher after he'd heard the boy's call. Right after Chris had been abandoned by his foster family in Tallahassee. The beginning of the partnership that had started this quest.

Page's brows rose. "Being a little defensive, aren't you?"

"I've seen this show before. Let's leave it at that and move on."

"Believe it or not, Mr. Weston, you're not the one we're interested in. You're just a sideshow. A very intriguing one, but a sideshow, nonetheless."

"Glad I could entertain you."

Kate said, "So who are you looking at for these murders?"

Kate thought she knew the answer, but wanted to hear it directly from the agents.

Page opened her mouth to reply, but the other agent finally spoke, cutting her off.

"We're not at liberty to identify suspects," he said. "Surely as a former police officer, you can appreciate our position. When was the last time you had contact with Judge Hoffman?"

Sinking back into her chair, Kate mulled the question. "A couple of years, at least. He retired long before I took over major crimes."

Page's partner gestured quote marks in the air. "Retired."

"That's what I said."

He crossed his arms over his chest. When he spoke, his words came out slowly, as if he were speaking to a child.

"Ms. Messenger, I know how to use a search engine. As soon as this guy came across our radar screen, I looked him up. The news articles didn't offer much detail, but I'm no idiot. I can read between the lines. The judge had a melt-down. He 'retired,'" again with the air quotes, "to avoid being thrown out."

Neither Kate nor Weston said anything.

"In addition to knowing how to use a search engine," the agent went on, "I can also use a telephone. I called the chairman of Judge Hoffman's party, the guy who was pushing for his ouster. He had all kinds of interesting anecdotes to share about Hoffman's behavior that last year or two."

The agent squeezed his eyes shut and massaged his temples.

"Let me see if I can remember this correctly. The guy used some colorful terms. Non-diagnostic, mind you, but colorful. Terms like 'stinking drunk' and 'batshit crazy.' Any of that ring a bell with you, Detective?"

Being referred to as "detective" jarred Kate. She guessed it was by design, as though he wanted her to remember what team she played for. Where her loyalties should lie.

Kate nodded. "I tried not to listen to the local scuttlebutt, but I know John had his problems. Some of them very public. Once his family left him, he spiraled down quickly. The change was pretty drastic. Screaming at people from the bench. A couple of drunk driving busts that got buried. And his neighbors reported him standing outside, yelling at the top of his lungs."

"Yelling?" Page asked. "At whom?"

Kate shrugged. "Not sure. I never scanned the reports firsthand. I just heard about them during shift briefings. But from what I understand, there wasn't anybody there."

Page raised an eyebrow. "Say again?"

"He was screaming at nothing. I'm guessing he was drunk. If his doctor put him on any medication and he was mixing that with alcohol…"

She let her words trail off.

She knew a little more, but decided to keep it to herself. In talking about this, a couple of additional details had surfaced. Probably nothing. But she kept them to herself.

"Did this surprise you?"

"Nothing surprises you once you've been a cop long enough. You two know that."

"Especially since they think they know everything," Weston said.

His words drew the agents' attention. Kate cleared her throat to draw them back to her. "But, yes, a judge standing outside his house, screaming, shook me a little."

"What did you make of it?" Page asked.

Kate shrugged again. "Look, I knew the guy. He helped me out a few times. But it wasn't like we were best friends or anything. I knew him through work and only barely so in that capacity. *You* two work together, and obviously travel together. Do you know everything about each other."

They ignored the question and Page's partner said, "Was Hoffman ever violent?"

Kate shook her head. "Not that I ever heard. Whenever the cops showed at his house, he went inside for the night and slept it off."

The partner pulled out a business card from inside his jacket and tossed it onto the table. "How long will you two be in town?"

"Not long," Weston said.

"That's unfortunate. Ms. Messenger, if you recall anything else, please call us." Kate acknowledged him with a nod. "Same for you, Mr. Weston."

Weston frowned at him.

"Not likely," he said.

12

WESTON UNLOCKED THE MOTEL ROOM door, pushed it open and gestured for Kate to go ahead. She moved inside. Christopher was seated on the edge of one of the beds, the television tuned to a game show. His pink photo album rested on the bed next to him.

Kate wondered if he'd had any luck communicating with Lucy, but even if he had, he might not share the news with them right away. She had learned that he was sometimes very cautious about sharing.

He turned his milky gaze toward the door and smiled.

You took a long time.

Weston walked between the twin beds and set his keys on a small nightstand positioned between them. He and the boy had their belongings in this room, while Kate was staying in an adjoining room.

"Sorry about that," Weston said. "We were... detained."

These were the first words he'd spoken since they'd left their impromptu meeting with the FBI.

They'd spent the ride back in silence. Weston, splotches of scarlet coloring his neck and cheeks, had seethed during the return trip, no doubt blaming Kate for the encounter.

For her part, Kate had found herself preoccupied with an unsettling memory.

She dropped into a chair and the boy looked at her.

Something's bothering you, Kate. What's wrong?

Kate shook her head. "I'm not sure."

"Well, I'm sure," Weston said. "Sure we have no business here. If the FBI thinks Hoffman is the Harbinger we *know* this is a fool's errand."

Kate said nothing. She had no appetite for more verbal sparring with Weston, and the truth was, she agreed. John Hoffman was surely in some kind of trouble, but he was not a serial killer who sent letters to the police. No amount of federal posturing could convince her of that. And the thought that Cindy Davis was sniffing around the same trail only sealed the deal.

Weston looked at her. "Like I said before, I'm sorry about your friend's struggle. But he's a goner, and now we're on the FBI's radar because of him. We need to get out of here and focus on finding the *real* Harbinger and hope he leads us to the Beast."

Kate sighed. "You're right," she said. "His methods may be completely different—and those photographs proved it— but the circumpunct on that letter has to mean something. And we need to know what. But we're not gonna find it here."

Weston looked mildly shocked. "So, we're in agreement on this?"

The cop in Kate hated like hell to walk away from Hoffman, but she had to think about the reason she'd joined Weston and Christopher in the first place. The Beast and anything potentially connected to him was the priority. Whatever trouble John was in, and no matter how wrong the FBI might be, he'd have to sort it all out himself. How many more people could die at the hands of a madman while the three of them spent their time trying to help someone who didn't appear to *want* anyone's help?

Hell, he wasn't even *that* much of a friend.

From the corner of her eye, she could see Weston looking at her.

She nodded. "John's on his own," she said. "And with the FBI running circles around him, that'll give us room to head down to Tallahassee and try to do what needs to be done. Why don't we get some food and sleep and leave first thing in the morning?"

Weston recovered from his shock and returned the nod, but if he considered this any type of victory, it wasn't showing on his face.

He just looked grim.

●

A few hours later, Kate was awakened by a voice in her head.

Jennifer wants us to stay.

Startled, she snapped bolt upright in bed, eyes open, heart slamming hard in her chest. Her first thought was of the Beretta hidden in her nightstand drawer, but then she saw Christopher's slim form standing next to her, silhouetted against the curtains that faced the lights of the parking lot.

Steadying herself, she reached over and flicked on a lamp. Christopher stared just past her shoulders, rubbing his hands over his arms.

"You scared me half to death," she said. "What are you doing up?"

Jennifer wants us to stay.

"Who?"

Jennifer.

Kate frowned. "Who's Jennifer?"

Arms still crossed over his chest, the boy shrugged his narrow shoulders and swayed side to side. Kate noticed his hair looked damp as if he'd been sweating. She set a hand on his forearm, which felt cold.

Maybe it was just the air conditioning.

His flesh twitched when her fingertips touched his skin, but he didn't recoil.

"Christopher? Who is Jennifer?"

I don't know.

"You don't know? She's communicating with you. How do you not know?"

She won't tell me.

Kate's eyes felt gritty from sleep and she rubbed at them to clear it away. "Where is this girl, Christopher? Or woman. Or whatever she is. Where did you talk to her?"

He continued to rock in place and a low moan escaped his lips.

Jesus, he seemed shook up. Sometimes he seemed so mature and capable, well beyond his years, but right now he looked like exactly what he was. An eleven-year-old boy.

"Do you need to sit?"

He shook his head.

"This Jennifer. Did she contact you?"

He nodded once.

"Okay, when? When did she contact you?"

Earlier.

"That's not very specific."

Earlier, he said again. *While you were out with Noah.*

"She came to the room?"

He shook his head and tapped an index finger against his temple.

She showed up here. In my head. Like Lucy used to. That's the second time.

Jesus Christ, Kate thought. "When was the first?"

At the restaurant. When I went blank. I just didn't know it then, but now I remember. It felt like a flood of feelings. And she's angry. Really angry.

Kate felt a chill. The first thing that came to mind was the *rusalka* they had encountered in Singer, but that was all over and done with.

"Why did she contact you, Chris? What does she want?"

From the corner of her eye, Kate saw something move. She glanced left and saw Weston standing in the doorway connecting their rooms. Weston's hair was mussed and he was dressed in a worn T-shirt and boxer shorts. She assumed he could hear the boy's thoughts, too.

"Come on, Chris," she said. "Tell me what she wants."

I did *tell you. She wants us to stay. Here in Apalache Springs.*

"I understand that. But *why?*"

He shrugged his shoulders.

Kate was beginning to feel exasperated. She'd gone to bed exhausted, and now she was wide awake in the middle of the night, scared half out of her wits, and being forced to play twenty questions.

Except she never got past the first two.

"There has to be a reason," she said.

She won't tell me. She just said we're supposed to meet someone.

Okay, now they were getting somewhere. Kate made a

conscious effort to keep the edge out of her voice when she spoke again. "Who are we supposed to meet?"

I don't know.

"Is she speaking to you now?"

A little.

Kate felt another chill. "What's she saying?"

Not saying. Showing.

Weston sucked in a sharp breath of air. "Okay, son, stay right where you are. I'll be back in a second."

Turning, he went into the other room. Kate heard him unzipping a duffel bag, followed by the sound of him rummaging around.

A few seconds later, he returned clutching his sketchpad and pencil. He looked around for a place to sit and Kate patted an empty space on her bed. He stared at it for a long moment, as though staring into a cobra's mouth.

She was about to tell him to grow up when he grunted and crossed to the nearest chair. Scooting it next to the bed, he dropped into it and opened the sketchpad on his lap.

"Send me whatever you can," he said to Chris.

Chris nodded, stared at the ceiling, and started rocking back and forth. Weston closed his eyes, his body going still except for the hand holding the pencil. He moved the tip rapidly across the paper.

Kate rose from the bed and went around behind Weston to stare over his shoulder. She was wearing only panties and a T-shirt with no bra, but figured this was not the time for modesty. Besides, Weston had zoned out.

He had already drawn an oval, and the guidelines for a face. As he filled in the features—a small nose, wide eyes, round cheeks and smooth forehead—she realized he was drawing a young girl of about seven or eight.

Kate knew that when Weston was done, the sketch's detail

would be rivaled only by a photograph. That, in itself, was amazing, but the fact that he admittedly had no artistic talent made it a miracle.

He was receiving the image from Christopher and translating it to the page.

Kate would've considered this impossible if she hadn't seen them do it before. Within the last several weeks, the impossible had become the norm.

As Weston drew, Christopher continued swaying, his milky eyes open and unblinking.

Weston was now using the pencil to shade the curve of the girl's forehead and had framed her face with long, straight hair. She looked cute yet unremarkable. Wide grin fronted by teeth still too big for her small mouth. Round cheeks and nose dotted with light brown freckles. A streak of dirt running over her chin.

But the eyes—wide and stained with terror—suddenly stabbed into Kate's heart like a long blade, triggering alternating waves of terror and rage.

The terror threatened to pull her under, made her legs unsteady and constricted her ribs, suffocating her. The rage was just as maddening, searing her insides, yet also weighing down her arms and legs, immobilizing her.

Jesus, she thought. What's happening to me?

She tore her gaze away from the picture, staggered to a nearby table and set both hands on it, using it for support.

The torrent of raw emotion mystified her. It struck her as if she were a child. Unfettered, unreasoning.

She couldn't pin it directly to anything from her own life. Had she tapped into something else? To Christopher? Or the girl in the picture?

Her chest loosened up and breathing came more easily.

Her legs steadied under her.

She pushed off from the table and turned toward the others. Hunched over the pad, Weston's hand glided across the page, the scratch of the pencil's tip against paper the only sound, Christopher rocking in place. Back and forth. Back and forth.

Kate bit her lower lip and moved back toward them. She had sensed something familiar about the girl's face, but didn't recognize her.

Swallowing hard, she chanced another look at the sketchpad. She again saw the rendering, the additional texture and shading giving the picture a lifelike quality.

This time, however, it triggered nothing in Kate, and she noticed that in one corner of the page, Weston had jotted "Sparkle."

He finished shading the girl's jaw, blinked twice, then came out of his trance and put the pencil down, staring at the drawing as if seeing it for the first time.

Kate gave him a sideways glance. "What does 'Sparkle' mean?"

He shook his head. "Hell if I know. Something must have compelled me to write it down, but I have no idea what it means."

"You capitalized it."

"Yeah."

"Is it a name?"

"The only people I know named Sparkle are strippers."

She raised an eyebrow. "You know strippers?"

He opened his mouth to speak, but was interrupted by the phone ringing in the other room.

He shot to his feet. "Who the hell could that be? It's the middle of the night."

He disappeared through the adjoining doorway. Kate pulled a pair of jogging shorts from her duffel, then slipped them on and turned to Christopher, who'd found his way to the bed and perched himself on its edge. She sat next to him and gently placed a hand on his forearm.

"Can you reach the girl now, Chris?"

He shook his head. In the silence, she could hear Weston's voice, though he spoke too softly for her to discern the words. She heard him return the phone receiver to its cradle.

"Do you know what Sparkle means?"

Another head shake, accompanied by a shrug.

Before she could press the issue, Weston returned to the room, his eyes narrowed and unfocused.

"Who was it?" she asked.

"Detective Miller, with a message for you."

"Miller? Why's he calling *your* room? And how did he even know I was here?"

"He said he tried several of the area motels and when the clerk heard your name, she put him through to me. I registered for both of us, remember?"

"And Miller couldn't have called my cell? What's the big emergency? What's this about?"

Weston opened his mouth to speak, hesitated, then said, "Judge Hoffman."

"What about him?"

Weston swallowed hard and stared at the floor. Kate could see the furrows in his forehead deepening and he seemed to be searching for the words.

"Damn it, Noah, what is it?"

"He's dead," Weston told her. "Judge Hoffman is dead."

13

KATE JUMPED TO HER FEET. "What do you mean he's dead? Was he in an accident?"

Weston heaved a sigh and shook his head. "Someone killed him."

"Killed him? What the hell? *Who*?"

"Your buddy Miller thinks it was the Harbinger."

Suddenly the room was swaying. Kate sat back down to steady herself. "Wait a minute, wait a minute. How does that make any sense? First the FBI practically broadcasts to us that they think *John* is the Harbinger, and now Miller thinks that's who *killed* him?"

"That's what he said."

"But the Harbinger goes after hookers, not men. And what about Tallahassee? That's where Chris thinks we'll find him."

Weston shrugged. "Maybe he's wrong. Maybe this is close enough. All I know is that Miller has questions and he wants us down at the scene."

•

It took about twenty minutes for them to get dressed and drive from their motel to the outskirts of town. As Weston drove, Kate sat in the passenger's seat, chewing her lip and trying to digest the news, Christopher quietly rocking on the seat behind her.

She saw the crime scene a block before they reached it. Or, more accurately, the red and blue flashing lights of the police cars.

"We may as well pull over here," she said. "They'll have the streets blocked so they can keep the gawkers and the news crews away. You said they found the body inside a house?"

Weston nodded. "But that's all I know."

He guided the station wagon to the curb, switched off the lights and killed the engine. Pocketing the keys, he glanced at Kate.

"You doing okay?" he asked.

Raking a hand through her hair, she nodded. "All things considered."

She popped open the door and exited the car as Weston told Chris to sit tight, then locked up and followed.

At the end of the block, they found a crowd of onlookers, most dressed in pajamas and bathrobes, others in T-shirts and shorts. With so many people home at this hour, it was possible one or more residents had heard something. But it was equally plausible that any noises had gone unnoticed.

Kate and Weston pushed into the crowd and worked their way through it. The police had lined up sawhorses to form a barricade.

When they reached one of the sawhorses, a burly cop with short black hair and a thick mustache gestured for them to halt.

"Detective Miller called us," Kate said and gave him their names.

"Are you family?"

She shook her head. The cop frowned and told them to hang on. He keyed his shoulder microphone, said a couple of numbers and waited for a response. Kate heard Miller's voice squawk in return.

"I have a Kate Messenger and a Noah Weston here," the cop said. "She says you wanted to see them."

"Send them back," Miller told him.

The cop pulled the sawhorse aside and let them through, jerking a thumb over his shoulder.

"242," he said. "Fourth house on the left. White aluminum siding. Don't step inside, it's a crime scene."

Kate nodded and started for the house, Weston by her side.

When they reached it, they found Miller standing on the front porch. His lips were pursed and his eyes were fixed on a spot on the ground. Kate couldn't tell for sure in the lighting, but she thought his face looked pale.

As she stepped onto the sidewalk, he looked up and the corners of his lips turned in a watered-down smile.

"Well, hey there," he said.

He stepped off the porch and moved their way. Pulling a cigarette from his shirt pocket, he slid it between his lips, torched the end with his lighter, then stuck a hand out to Weston.

"Nice to put a face to the voice on the phone," he said.

Weston eyed him warily, but shook the hand as Kate nodded toward the house.

"Is John in there?" she asked.

"He is."

"Can you tell us what happened?"

"What happened is someone carved him up. Gutted the poor bastard."

Kate felt lightheaded. Sucked in a lungful of air to steady herself.

She'd seen her share of corpses, people who had died horribly. But it always hit her differently when it was someone she knew.

She stared at the house. The mailbox was overstuffed, and rolled-up newspapers littered the porch. Grass stood at least a couple feet high and tangles of weeds had overtaken the flower beds. Papers adorned with official-looking seals and business logos were taped to the front storm door.

"Vacant," Miller said. "It's a rental house, but it's been empty for months now. Some out-of-town company owns it, from what the neighbors say."

Weston swept his gaze over the neighborhood. "Nobody heard anything?"

"Not a damn thing."

"Seems hard to believe."

The detective shrugged, took a drag off his cigarette. "I have two detectives canvassing and people swear they heard nothing."

"Maybe they don't want to get involved," Weston said.

Miller smirked. "This place? These people call us once a week, bitch about this empty house and demand extra patrols. You'd think there was a fucking al Qaeda training camp in the basement or something."

"How do you know someone didn't kill John and dump him here?" Kate asked.

"I don't. But it seems damn unlikely, since at least two of the neighbors swear they saw him drive up in his Caddie, park it, and walk the neighborhood."

"Why was he walking the neighborhood?"

"Looking for a liquor store?"

Miller grinned, amused by his own humor.

Kate felt her face burn hot. "Did you drag us out of bed for us to listen to this bullshit?"

"The lady has a point," Weston said. "It's late and you called us. I'm assuming you had a reason for that. If you thought we were involved you wouldn't have called us out here. There'd be a couple of your detectives rousting us at the motel right now, asking for permission to search our room."

Miller nodded. "What happened in there is carnage, like something out of a damned slasher movie. You two didn't do that. I'm no psychologist, but I know people."

"You don't know me," Weston said.

"No, but I had a nice sit down with Kate, here, and she strikes me as a woman of character. And I don't care what some bloated district attorney up in North Carolina says about you, he's got a shit case, and I just can't see Kate shacking up with a man who butchered his own family." He smiled. "But I may be alone in that opinion."

So he'd spoken to the FBI, probably not long after their encounter with Agent Page and her partner at Hoffman's motel.

Not much of a surprise.

"Which brings us back to our original question," Kate said. "Why did you call us?"

Miller dropped his cigarette and ground it under the toe of his shoe.

"Pretty simple. After his attorney paid his bail and Hoffman picked up his belongings, he happened to mention to a clerk that he was in a hurry because he had to meet with his old friend Kate at his motel. Turns out the clerk couldn't sleep, heard his name on a late night news bulletin and was smart enough to give us a jingle."

Kate said, "We never met up with him, if that's the question."

"But I know you at least tried to, so the question is this: did he ever call you after you left his motel?"

"You couldn't have asked me this over the phone?"

"Like I said, I know people. But I like to look 'em in the eye when they answer."

Kate shook her head. She couldn't be sure the message she'd listened to was from Hoffman. "Never," she said. "And when he was a no-show, I assumed he'd left town. Especially with the FBI sniffing around."

Miller snorted. "Those tight-lipped sonsabitches thought they had their man." He gestured toward the house. "But this shit's a goddamned thunderstorm on their little parade. They're back to square one."

Kate nodded. "So, what makes you think this Harbinger killer is good for this?"

"Because I've seen what's in there, and I figure it's his way of telling the task force to go fuck themselves. They had the wrong guy."

"Helluva a way to set them straight," Weston said.

"You're telling me." Miller looked at Kate. "I tried to contact Hoffman's attorney, but she isn't answering her phone. Did he have any next of kin?"

"Around here?" Kate asked. "I'm not sure. But his wife and two children disappeared somewhere here in Florida several years ago."

Miller's brows arched. "Disappeared? Disappeared how?"

"As in gone. The three of them left to spend a month down here and never came home. No contact after the fact.

They were just..." Kate's voice trailed off as she searched for the words. "They were just gone."

"Was he smacking them around?"

"I don't think so. From what I could tell, they seemed happy."

"The rich abusers, they know how to make it look good. It's always one big happy family. Everybody smiling while the wife and kids are getting the crap kicked out of them. We both know that."

Kate nodded. "That's not how it was with John, though. We weren't best buddies, but I know he doted on his children. They never seemed intimidated by him. Same for his wife." She paused. "Is there a reason you think this is relevant?"

Miller heaved a sigh and reached for another cigarette. "No. Just trying to understand why he was here or what he was looking for. He say anything about that?"

"Nothing," Kate lied.

John had clearly mentioned his kids, but her gut told her to keep that bit of information to herself. She wasn't sure why.

His cigarette lit, Miller blew a plume of smoke from the corner of his mouth. "How much longer are you two in town?"

"We were planning to leave this morning," Weston said.

"That a fact?"

"It is."

"And you're going where?"

"Away."

Miller frowned. "That narrows it down."

"If you need anything," Kate said, "you have my cell number. I'm still not sure why you didn't call that instead of the motel."

"I did and got sent straight to voice mail."

She frowned, and then it hit her. "Ahh, right," she said, and felt a little embarrassed. She'd left her phone on the nightstand and had forgotten to plug it into the charger.

"Just one more question before I let you two go."

Miller pulled a small notebook from his khaki pants, flipped through several pages until he found what he was looking for, then turned it toward Kate and Noah. On the page was a crudely drawn circle with a dot inside it.

"I don't know how much you folks know about the Harbinger, but does this mean anything to you?"

Before Kate could speak, Weston said, "No."

Miller showed it to Kate. "What about you? Mean anything?"

She shook her head. "Should it?"

"No, but it never hurts to ask. For all I know it might have some connection to Hoffman."

Kate and Weston exchanged a look.

"Why would you think that?" she asked.

"This thing's already been leaked all over the Internet, so I guess it doesn't hurt to tell you. It's the symbol the Harbinger put on a letter he sent to the task force. One of the guys on my squad says it's a religious mark. The God Ra, or some shit."

"And what's that got to do with John?"

"Good question," he said. "But it's spray-painted on the wall inside the house."

14

BY THE TIME THEY STARTED BACK toward the Rambler, the crowd had thinned.

Kate figured a few of the more morbid residents would loiter around until the cops wheeled out the body on a stretcher and loaded it into the coroner's wagon. Most would decide they'd rather call it a night and go to sleep. Or at least go home and take sneak peeks through their curtains to watch without feeling so ghoulish about it.

As they walked, Kate's throat ached dully and she felt a weight on her chest, making it hard to breathe. She was upset that Hoffman, once a decent man, had ended his life mentally and physically broken. That he'd died so horribly only compounded her grief.

But that wasn't the only thing weighing her down. The spray-painted circumpunct was uppermost in her mind, cementing the notion that the Beast might've had a hand in this.

Or did it?

The Harbinger's letter had been leaked on the web and had surely gone viral by now. Not only that, the symbol was common enough that a quick Internet search revealed its ancient history and the various meanings assigned to it, so it wasn't exactly an unknown entity.

More importantly, the Beast was not known to spray paint signs on the walls of his crime scenes. In their experience, he seemed content to remain anonymous, not interested in announcing his presence beyond the simple taking of his victims' tongues—which might explain how he'd managed to stay active for so many years.

So, when it came down to it, Miller could be right that the Harbinger was behind John's murder. But again, the victim here was not a hooker—the Harbinger's usual prey—and the idea that he would kill a potential suspect to send a message to the task force seemed like a stretch to Kate. Something out of a bad TV movie.

But what if someone else, someone who had seen the Harbinger's letter on the Internet and held a personal grudge against Hoffman, had used the circumpunct in an attempt to point the cops in the wrong direction?

This wouldn't be the first time Kate had seen such a scenario, and it was the one that made the most sense to her.

Weston suddenly cleared his throat and she expected him to weigh in on this, but he surprised her by saying, "I'm sorry, Kate. I'm sorry about your friend."

His voice was soft, infused with a gentleness he usually reserved for Christopher. Was it the voice he had used to soothe his wife and children when they were hurt or upset?

"Thank you," she said.

"I've been thinking about that symbol on the wall. And as much as I'd like it to be a signpost pointing directly at the Beast—or even the Harbinger—my gut tells me it's neither one."

"You've been reading my mind."

He smiled. "I'm afraid that's Christopher's territory, not mine. You have any idea what might have happened?"

She shook her head. "None. John wasn't Mr. Popularity back home. But we're not there now. I can't see why someone would do this to him."

"Is it possible he got drunk, shot off his mouth, and someone decided to teach him a lesson?"

"Anything's possible. But like Miller said, what happened back there wasn't just a murder. You don't carve someone up over a bar fight. That was rage."

"What kind of ties did Hoffman have in Florida?"

Kate shrugged. "I've got no clue. He told me he was here to fix something and mentioned his children, but that's all I know. And other than the police, the only person I've seen him have contact with is his lawyer."

"What do you know about her?"

"Just her name. Angela Lowenthal."

"Either way, like I said, she reeked of money and I can't see how Hoffman could afford much more than a bottle of Two Buck Chuck. So *something* was going on there."

As they got close to the Rambler, they saw that Christopher had stepped out and was leaning against the seam between the door and the quarter panel.

He turned his blind eyes toward them and acknowledged them with a nod.

His ability to identify them without the benefit of sight still unnerved Kate. She understood that losing a sense heightened the others, but this was something far different.

And if he was *that* powerful, *that* tuned into them, what else could he do?

Weston said, "You should've stayed in the car, Chris."

I wasn't getting anything from in there.

"Are you getting something now?"

He nodded. *The judge wasn't afraid. Kate, you need to know that. He was hurting. Emotionally. Physically. He was sad, but not afraid.*

That stopped Kate in her tracks. "Are you sure?"

Yes. But I can feel rage, too. So much rage.

"That would track with the way he was killed," Weston said. "Whoever killed him had to be out of his mind with rage."

Her mind, Chris said.

"It was a woman?"

Yes.

He squeezed his eyes closed and covered them with his hands. He cocked his head to one side, like a dog trying to listen to a high-frequency sound only it could hear.

No, wait, their *minds.*

"Two people?"

Yes.

"Who?"

She won't say. She doesn't trust you. Not yet.

Kate moved forward and put a hand on his shoulder. "What are you talking about, Chris? *Who* won't say?"

He didn't respond.

"Do you mean Jennifer? Is she back?"

Yes, he said, but the word sounded distant. Little more than an echo inside Kate's head.

Eyes closing, Chris's lips began to move, as though he was speaking to someone. Just like in the diner. His brow furrowed and he began gesturing with his hands, something he rarely did.

"Chris?" Kate squeezed his shoulder to try to reach him, but got no response.

Without warning, a cold, terrible sensation pierced Kate's gut, causing her to shudder. Her heart revved up, slamming so hard inside her chest she swore it would explode, and blood thundered in her ears. She wanted to scream, but her vocal cords and tongue wouldn't respond.

Tears stung the corners of her eyes and her vision blurred. Her breath began coming in ragged gasps and she felt as though some unseen force was literally sucking the oxygen from her lungs.

Kate plummeted to her knees, only vaguely aware of someone shouting her name.

Weston? She had no way of knowing for sure.

A high-pitched voice—a little girl's voice—boomed in her head, the sound tunneling through her brain like the point of a red-hot drill bit.

Hands off, cunt. He doesn't belong to you!

Kate pitched forward onto all fours.

Her throat began to close and she could no longer draw in air. Black spots danced in her vision as she struggled to catch her breath.

Oh, Christ. Oh, Jesus, she was here on the ground, dying, and she had no idea how or why. Her limbs grew weak. Her eyes wanted to close and she couldn't stop them. The inevitability of it all overtook her. Her will evaporated.

Her body was shutting down and she had no way of stopping it.

How do you fight what you can't see? What you can't punch or shoot?

These were her last thoughts before she blacked out.

15

WHEN KATE'S EYES FLUTTERED OPEN, the first thing she saw was Weston looming over her, his face etched with worry.

"Jesus, are you all right?"

"I don't know," she said. "I think so."

She shifted onto her side and paused. Her stomach rolled and lightheadedness overtook her. She clamped her eyes shut and tried to ride it out. As it subsided, she became aware of Weston's hand resting on her upper arm, not heavily, just enough that she knew he was there.

She sat up and took a couple of deep breaths, waiting for the dizziness to subside. Then she looked at Weston. "That was really horrible. What the hell just happened?"

"You tell me," he said. "One minute, you were standing there. Then you touched Christopher, screamed, and went down."

Kate heard footsteps coming from the direction of the house where Hoffman had been murdered. She looked past Weston and grimaced. A couple of paramedics were running toward her.

"Ma'am, are you all right?" one of them shouted.

"I'm fine," she said, trying to dismiss him with a wave.

His partner, a stocky black man, gave Weston a questioning glance.

Weston said, "If the woman says she's fine, she's fine. She knew the victim in that house and she's a little shook up. It's just stress."

"Are you sure?" he asked.

"Really," Weston said, "she just needs some rest. This has been a nasty surprise for her."

The first paramedic was now squatting next to Kate. He asked if he could do a quick check of her vitals and she agreed. He checked her heart and her pulse, looked into her eyes with a penlight, and performed a couple other tests.

He stood and said, "Her husband's right. She seems fine."

Nobody bothered to correct him.

The stocky one had been eyeing Chris, who was again leaning against the car, brooding.

"What about this young man?" he asked. "He's sweating like crazy."

Weston flashed the paramedics a disarming smile. "It's just the heat and humidity. He's fine, too."

"He acts like he hasn't noticed us."

"He's blind," Weston said. "And quiet around strangers. But he's fine." He gestured toward Kate with his chin. "She's the one who took the fall."

The stocky one opened his mouth to speak, but his partner cut him off. "Mike, the lady checks out, so why don't we let these folks go home for the night?"

His expression uncertain, the stocky one registered his agreement with an almost imperceptible nod. By the time they'd taken off, Kate had risen to her feet.

She gave Weston a tight smile. "Wow. You were almost charming."

"Don't get used to it."

"Heaven forbid."

She turned to Christopher, who was still leaning against the Rambler. Sweat had darkened his shirt, pressing it against his slim frame, and his bangs hung in dark tendrils over his forehead.

How are you feeling? he asked.

"I'm okay now, but what just happened, Chris? I heard a little girl's voice in my head and she sounded pretty angry. Was it Jennifer?"

Yes.

"She tried to hurt me."

I know. I'm sorry. I tried to tell her to stop.

"Who *is* she, Chris?"

I told you before, she won't say.

"You aren't holding out on us, are you? Like you did with Lucy?"

Lucy's gone.

"I know that. And you'll find her again, I'm sure you will. But I need to know about Jennifer. Are you holding out on us or not?"

He shook his head. *No.*

Kate felt conflicted, not sure she believed him, but hoping it wasn't a lie. Patience had never been her strong suit, and after what had just happened to her, it wasn't easy to stop herself from calling him out. She clenched her jaw, shook her head, then moved past him and climbed into the

Rambler.

"Let's go," she said.

It took all of her will to stop herself from slamming the door.

16

THE RAPPING OF KNUCKLES AGAINST the motel room door pulled Kate from sleep.

Her eyes popped open and she glanced at the clock. 7:30. Too early for housekeeping.

She cast aside her sheet, sat up, and threw her legs over the edge of the bed. She and the guys had returned only two hours ago and her head hurt from lack of sleep.

The frenetic knocking wasn't helping a damn bit.

"Hang on," she shouted.

She got up, crossed the room, then peered through the peephole and swore under her breath.

The FBI agents they'd encountered yesterday stood outside her room.

She crossed and closed the adjoining door, so as not to disturb Chris and Weston, and when she pulled open the front door, a wave of moist, hot air hit her in the face. The smell of sun-heated garbage from a Dumpster, combined with diesel exhaust and cologne. She threw the door open wide, knowing the agents would be looking past her to check out her room.

"Did we wake you?" Agent Page asked.

Kate ignored the question. "Can I help you two?"

"May we come in?"

She stepped clear of the doorway and gestured for them to step inside. Fortunately, Weston had cleaned up his sketch-pad and pencil from last night's impromptu art session.

Agent Page came in, followed by her partner. The card he'd left during their earlier encounter had said his name was Jefferson. Kate shut the door behind them and pulled open the curtains, filling the room with sunlight.

"I suppose you know why we're here," Jefferson said.

Kate ignored him. The room had a four-cup drip coffee maker and she began rummaging through a pile of pre-measured packets of coffee, sugar, creamer and plastic stir sticks. Flipping open the basket, she inserted a coffee packet, shut the basket and hit the power button. She'd filled the reservoir with water the night before.

The coffee pot gurgled and she turned toward the two agents.

Jefferson stood near the door, coat folded over one arm, and dabbed sweat from his scalp with a white handkerchief.

Page stood a few feet from Kate, her legs spread slightly apart, fists cocked on her hips. All she needed was a red cape.

"You look tired," she said.

Kate detected no concern in her voice. "Sorry about the puffy eyes. I'll smear some hemorrhoid cream under them a little later and they'll be good as new."

She turned her gaze to Agent Jefferson.

"Did you two wake me up to tell me I look tired or is there an actual fucking reason for this visit?"

Jefferson smirked. "Not much for mornings, are you?"

"Hectic night," she said.

By now the coffee was ready. She poured some into a foam cup and turned back toward the agents. She brought it to her lip and stared at them over its rim as she blew on the coffee to cool it.

Her visitors had fallen silent, which didn't surprise Kate. She continued to blow on her coffee and kept her eyes fixed on a spot on the wall.

Finally, Jefferson cleared his throat. "Like I said, I suppose you know why we're here."

She flashed a weak smile and shrugged.

He licked his lips. "Hoffman's dead. You're aware of that, right?"

She nodded. "The locals called me out to the scene last night. But I assume you already knew that."

Page frowned. "It seems odd. You and your traveling companion come here and suddenly Hoffman's dead."

Kate nodded and sipped her coffee.

"So you agree?" Page asked.

"Hoffman being dead isn't odd. That's just unfortunate. That he was gutted by some lunatic in an abandoned home, that's odd. That he was considered a person of interest in a serial case, yet ended up with his guts carved out, that's odd. Frankly, I'd consider it tragic. But you two are the professionals here."

She downed more coffee.

"Where were you last night?" Jefferson asked.

"Here."

"Can someone verify that?"

"Weston."

Page smirked. "A guy who may have butchered his own family? He's your alibi? Maybe we should ask the blind kid, too."

"His name's Christopher."

"Right."

"And maybe you *should* question him. Maybe you think *he* killed Judge Hoffman."

"Detective..." Jefferson said.

He was doing it again. "I'm not a detective."

"Obviously," Page said.

"Sorry," Jefferson continued. "Ms. Messenger. Why did you and Mr. Weston come to Florida? I mean, really?"

"I told you, I knew the judge—"

"—and you wanted to help the poor old drunk, right?" The corners of Jefferson's thin lips turned up in a smile. "Ms. Messenger, Kate, that all sounds great. Very altruistic. But I'm just having trouble wrapping my mind around it. You can appreciate that, can't you? I mean, why are you even on this side of the country?"

"Because I resigned from the department and felt like traveling a little. Is there something wrong with that?"

Sweat had beaded on Jefferson's scalp. He sopped up the perspiration with his handkerchief and studied the cloth for several seconds, his lower lip protruding slightly.

"We've established that you left the police department," he said. "Agent Page talked to one of your former coworkers yesterday."

"Oh? Who?"

"Sergeant Bob MacLean," Page said.

Shit, Kate thought. Here we go again.

"Fascinating guy," Page continued, and Kate could hear the taunt in her voice. "He had some interesting information to share regarding you and your... departure."

Even on his best days, MacLean was a horse's ass on steroids. But when Kate had beaten him out of a promotion and took command of the major crimes division, he'd done everything he could to undermine her. When she'd booted him out of the division altogether, things had only gotten worse.

So, yeah, she guessed MacLean had spouted all sorts of interesting things about her, just as he had to Ms. Cindy Davis, her favorite news hack. Some of them may have even been true, though she doubted it.

"I can only imagine," she said.

Something flickered in Agent Page's eyes and Kate could tell that she'd already made up her mind about her. "You two didn't get along well."

"We both wanted the same job. I got it. He didn't. I became his boss. It caused friction."

Page responded with a small nod.

"Well, apparently it worked out for him," she said. "He's still a detective. He even got your old job. The one you left."

Her gut churning, Kate said nothing.

"So, tell me. Why does a woman like you, the daughter of a cop and a dispatcher, work so hard, get what she wants and give it up?"

Kate forced a smile. "Is this leading somewhere?"

"Your traveling companion," Page said. "MacLean told me you took him into custody back in Santa Flora and held him for almost twenty-four hours. So you must've had some doubts about him yourself. Is that true?"

"Yes."

"Yet here you are."

"Because it was all bullshit. He didn't kill his family."

"And you know that how?"

Kate chewed at her lip and with her free hand brushed some loose strands of hair from her face.

What could she say?

There was evidence that had exonerated the man, and Kate's gut—her intuition—told her he was innocent. Despite his grim disposition, all she'd witnessed since she'd met Weston and Christopher told her to trust them. Yet here she was, unable to explain any of it.

Page cleared her throat. "How can you be so sure he didn't kill them?"

"We've been over this, already," Kate said. "The forensics report cleared him. And he had an alibi. A witness."

Page snorted. "Right. A woman he was sleeping with—which sounds like a very good motive for murdering your wife. Even your kids. Maybe they'd all become inconvenient for him. And we both know that the lack of conclusive DNA isn't really proof of anything."

Kate said nothing. She turned and poured herself more coffee.

Jefferson said, "Kate, we know there have been others."

Tensing, she slowly lowered the coffee pot and turned toward the agents, both of whom were staring at her.

"Other murders," Jefferson said.

"Hoffman?"

Jefferson shook his head. "Not Hoffman. The murders in North Carolina? Weston's family? The tongues were cut out, right?"

"Yes."

"You know they found another family in Tacoma who'd been through the same thing. Sliced up. Tongues cut out of their mouths before the killer burned their house down. Horrible shit." He paused. "Judging by your expression, you already knew that."

"I did."

"You know Weston was in Tacoma, right?"

"Yes."

"You know why?"

"No idea. He's been lots of places."

"Right," Jefferson said. "Traveling in that crappy station wagon, hauling around the kid. That alone is weird enough."

Kate's stomach knotted. She noticed her jaw was clenched so tightly her back teeth were beginning to throb.

"See, here's the point," Page said. "You can dance around it any way you want, but your friend's a person of interest. He was never charged, but that doesn't mean authorities in North Carolina don't still consider him a suspect. Their *prime* suspect. You get that, right? You get he was never cleared in a court of law."

Kate opened her mouth to answer, but Jefferson cut her off, directly addressing Page. "Of course, she knows that. She's a cop. Or she used to be. She knows the score."

"Look," Page said, "you know about the killings in North Carolina and Tacoma, but did you know there were other victims in other states? Families? Slaughtered? The body count's stunning. Women, children. There's a monster out there."

When Kate spoke, she had to force the words through clenched teeth. "How high is it? The body count, I mean?"

"Damn high," Page said. "We're not ready to give a number, but it's high. Trust us on that. Which, again, begs the question, why does a former detective quit her job to tour the country with a mass murderer?"

"Noah's not a mass—"

"You're a groupie," Page said. "For a goddamn serial killer."

"He's not a killer, damn it!" The words came out as a

shout.

"Look, we have a maniac on the loose in Florida. We have another one crisscrossing the country, murdering entire families. And here's little Kate, standing in the middle of it all."

"And yesterday you were pretty much shouting that you thought Judge Hoffman was the Harbinger. You don't know what you're talking about."

"Don't I? We heard you had daddy issues, Kate."

Kate frowned. "Where the hell did you hear that?"

"Bob MacLean."

"And how the hell would he know anything about my father and me?"

Page smiled. "He told me he got drunk with your ex-hubby one night and the ex spilled it all. How dear old daddy treated you like a leper and you never forgave him for it. And then you quit the force and took up with a murder suspect."

Kate couldn't believe what she was hearing. Dan was a cheating bastard, but how could he have betrayed her like that? And that asshole Bob MacLean needed a beat down something fierce.

"Fuck MacLean," she spat. "Fuck both of them."

Jefferson's brows went up. "Speaking of which, is that what this is about? Are you fucking Weston? Maybe Agent Page is onto something with this groupie thing. Are you one of his Manson girls or something?"

Page snorted again and shot Jefferson a look. "Maybe the psycho gutted Hoffman to show off a little. Or maybe he didn't feel like competing for her affection."

Kate slammed her cup down on the nearest table. Brown liquid sloshed over the rim of the cup, hot enough to sting the skin of her thumb. She barely felt it. She had too much

EDWARD FALLON

adrenaline coursing through her body to notice.

She took a step toward Page and Jefferson.

"I don't give a damn what you think about me," she said, her finger jabbing into the air between her and Page. "But you are completely out of your depth with all of this. Noah Weston is *not* a..."

She heard the rattle of a doorknob and whipped around as Weston opened the adjoining door.

Shit.

He had slipped on a pair of jeans and a black T-shirt. His hair was tousled and his feet bare. His eyes were narrow slits, his cheeks bright red, his voice loud and angry. "What the hell's going on in here?"

"They were just leaving," Kate said.

Page shook her head. "Bullshit, we aren't done yet."

Weston took a step forward. "You are as far as we're concerned. Get out. Now."

Jefferson held up his hands in a gesture of surrender. "No need to get riled up, tough guy. We can take a hint."

"And yet here you stand." The volume had drained from Weston's voice, but Kate still detected a hint of menace.

Page glared at him before turning to Kate. "The next conversation won't be so pleasant."

"Yeah," Kate said. "This was a regular damn tea party."

Her gaze returning to Weston, Page backed toward the door, which Jefferson was opening, then slammed it behind her as she exited.

17

WESTON GLOWERED AT KATE. "What in Christ's name was that all about?"

"They were asking me about you," she said. "About what happened to your family. And that family up in Tacoma. And about why I left my job in Santa Flora."

"And what did you tell them?"

"Nothing," she said. She forced the word through clenched teeth, making it sound like a hiss. "I told them they were full of shit."

"And?"

"They think *I'm* full of shit."

"Morons."

Adrenaline coursing through her system, Kate took another step forward. "*Are* they morons?"

Her heart slammed in her chest and her fingers curled into

fists. She noticed Weston's body stiffen as she closed in on him.

"*Are* they morons, Noah? I'm in here telling them you're not some nutcase who cuts people's tongues out, then you take it on yourself to burst into the room like some crazy man and throw them out."

"You said they were leaving, I decided to help them along."

"And now you've pissed them off."

"*Me*? I didn't wake up because you were all singing *Kumbaya*."

Kate sighed. He was right. She was the one who had started shouting. They had played her like the experts they were and she had taken the bait.

She should have known better. But Weston sure hadn't helped the situation.

"Maybe they'll let it go for now," she said. "But sooner or later they'll be back, and they could detain us and drag us off for questioning."

"Wonderful. You know, Chris and I did a pretty good job of staying under the radar until you came along."

"I was invited, remember? If you still have a problem with it, talk to our little friend." She paused. "We'd better start packing."

Weston shook his head. "We can't. Not now."

"What are you talking about? I know John's murder threw a monkey wrench into things, but we need to get out of here."

"You're not making sense."

"Do the math. There's a murderer on the loose. You are a person of interest in a homicide case in North Carolina. Since we've arrived in town, a man I know—a man *they* believed was the Harbinger—has been brutally murdered, and they're dumb enough to think *you* did it."

"Which is exactly why we can't leave. I know I'm always the one who wants to cut and run, but that'll just make them more suspicious, and I've got enough clouds hanging over my head." He paused and took a breath. "Besides, I did some thinking before I fell asleep. You remember what Chris said about Hoffman's murder right before you blacked out? I know you've been rattled, but—"

"That there were two of them. Two people who killed him. And at least one of them was female."

"Exactly," Weston said. "And maybe if we can figure out who they are, that'll put us right with the FBI."

Kate snorted. "You're joking, right? Those two make Bob MacLean look like a fucking genius."

"We have to at least try," he said. "I don't see any other way."

"You don't think they'll be watching us?"

"I think you're probably a good enough cop to know when they are. We'll just have to be careful."

She nodded. "Maybe Sergeant Miller can help us. He has as much use for the Feds as we do, and I'm guessing he'll stonewall them and hang onto this case as long as he can."

"But Miller also thinks the Harbinger is good for Hoffman's murder."

"Yeah, but he's the only cop around who believes you're an innocent man. I don't have to tell him what we're up to. Just use him for information."

"Good point."

She glanced at the clock. "He probably pulled an all-nighter at the crime scene. I'll call the station and see if he's come back yet."

"Wouldn't he be home in bed by now?"

"Maybe, but they're not a large department and he's a

supervisor. He'd have to make sure all the evidence was bagged, tagged, and locked up before he clocks out. You can't just hand it off to the next shift."

"Call him." Weston said.

Kate crossed to the nightstand and snatched up her cell phone. Fortunately, she'd started charging it as soon as she got back to the room.

She dialed Miller, and by the fourth ring, she thought she might get dumped into voice mail, but he finally answered.

"Miller."

"It's Kate."

"Ms. Messenger, how's it going?"

"I'm guessing you pulled an all-nighter?"

"I did."

"Did I catch you in bed?"

"Not even close. I'm probably still a couple hours away from hitting the sack."

"Still bagging and tagging?"

"I'm about to make a run to Hoffman's motel room, see what I can find out there."

This was perfect, Kate thought. "Would you mind if I came by and had a look?"

"Why?"

"You know how it is. When I get back to California, they'll grill me about everything. I just want to make sure I don't miss anything, especially since this has turned into a murder investigation."

"Come on, Kate. How naive do you think I am? The Feds told me about your friend, you think they didn't tell me about you? You lied to me with all that Santa Flora County crap."

"So why didn't you mention that this morning?"

"Because I stand by my feeling that you're good people,

and it isn't really pertinent to my investigation. All that mattered was what you could tell me about the judge."

Kate felt a little guilty for holding back on him. "Yeah, well I'm sorry about the lying part, but I saw a friend in distress and thought it was the easiest way to get information."

"I figured as much," Miller said.

"And that's all this is right now. The cop in me thinking about a friend. So what do you say?"

Miller was quiet for several seconds and she assumed he was considering the request.

He sighed. "All right, I guess it couldn't hurt to give you a quick tour. But you know the rules. Don't touch or take anything without telling me."

"That works. I'll see you in a bit."

She clicked off. She doubted she'd actually find anything at Hoffman's motel room, but it would give her a chance to talk with Miller a bit more, and maybe he'd be able to fill in some blanks. She could hope, anyway.

She turned and found Weston gone.

She'd taken three steps toward the adjoining door when he started shouting for her.

18

KATE RAN INTO THEIR ROOM and found Christopher still in bed, Noah kneeling next to him.

Chris was curled up on the mattress, his frail form making a small lump beneath the covers. The back of his head and the sole of an exposed foot were the only parts of him that were visible.

Kate noted that his body was covered not only with a sheet and bedspread, but also with two more blankets.

Even with the air conditioner laboring, the room felt warm and stuffy. Why was he covered in blankets?

When she got close enough, she heard small moans emanating from him and saw tremors passing through his body. His eyes were squeezed shut and sweat had beaded on his forehead.

"How long's he been like this?"

"I'm not sure," Weston said. "I figured he was just cold."

"Cold? You're kidding, right?"

Kate pushed past Weston so she could get closer to the boy. She reached down and gently pressed a hand over his forehead. His skin felt moist from perspiration, but also icy.

"Jesus. He *is* cold. Really cold."

"That's why I shouted for you."

Lifting her hand from Chris's forehead, she set it on his shoulder and shook him. "Christopher, are you all right?"

His eyes stayed screwed shut. He drew his legs up closer to his chest and groaned. Kate shook him twice more, harder each time, but he didn't stir.

Weston cursed under his breath. Pushing past her, he rolled the boy onto his back, shook him and said his name in a sharp, loud voice.

Christopher didn't respond. His body trembled. Weston pulled the covers back up around the boy's neck. He looked at Kate, worry etched on his features. "What the hell's going on with him?"

"I don't know," she said. "Was he like this when you got up this morning?"

"He was curled up like that, but I assumed he was just asleep. And I was too distracted by all the shouting in your room to pay much attention to him."

"We should take him to a doctor," she said.

"And say what? I've known this kid for awhile now and he never gets sick. Never. And I can almost guarantee you this isn't something a doctor could fix."

"Then what the hell is it?"

"I don't know, but if I have to guess, I'm betting it has something to do with that girl he's in contact with. You said she hurt you last night. Maybe she's hurting him now."

"Maybe you're right, but I'd still feel better if we—"

Christopher groaned suddenly. His eyes cracked open.

Weston blew out a relieved breath and rested a hand on the boy's shoulder. "Hey, kid, how are you?"

Cold.

"Don't worry," Kate said. "We're gonna get you some help."

Don't need help. Need sleep. Need another blanket.

"You need a doctor," Kate said.

He shook his head.

No, no doctors.

He rested a hand on Weston's forearm and squeezed.

No doctors. You have to trust me on this. Please. No doctors. No hospitals. It's not that kind of problem.

"Is it Jennifer again? Is she hurting you?"

He didn't answer.

"Chris," Kate said. "Can you hear us?"

Yes, but you need to leave me alone and let me sleep. I'll get better. I promise. If you take me to a doctor, he'll poke and prod me. He'll see what the Beast did to me and probably call the police. You know he will. No doctors. No hospitals. Please.

His eyes closed and his breathing grew deeper.

"We need to call 911," Kate said.

Weston rose from the bed. "No. He says he doesn't want a doctor. We should respect that."

"We can't let a kid make that kind of decision."

"What the hell are you talking about? We're all here *together* because of the decisions he's made. He's the engine that runs this little bus."

"I get that. But this is different. He's in distress. He needs help."

Weston sighed. "Look. I understand you're concerned. I am, too. But he seems to know what he's dealing with, and who knows, maybe he's dealt with it before. Before either of us met him. So whatever it is, we let him ride it out."

"I can't stand here and watch him like this."

"Then don't," Weston said. "Go meet up with Miller. Do what you need to do. I'll stay here, and trust me, if he gets any worse you'll know about it."

Kate's heart was pounding. "I don't want to leave him, either."

"He'll be fine. I'm sure of it. And if he isn't, I don't think there's a goddamned doctor on the planet who can do anything about it. Now go."

Kate looked at Chris, asleep but looking miserable, then shifted her gaze to Weston. She knew he was as torn by this as she was, but it didn't show on his face.

"Go," he said.

So she did.

19

KATE PARKED THE RAMBLER OUTSIDE Hoffman's motel.

She sat with the engine running, staring at the dilapidated building, but barely able to concentrate. All she could think about was Christopher, lying on that bed, looking so fragile.

She had no children of her own, and she was an only child, so no nieces or nephews, either. When she and Dan were married they had both led busy lives and having kids had never been a priority for either of them.

But as much as Christopher's power scared her at times, she couldn't help feeling protective of the boy. And if something were to happen to him...

She sat there for a long moment, looking now at the white Ford sedan parked near the motel office that screamed of cop and knew it had to be Miller's car. She wondered if she should simply turn around and go back to her motel.

But what would that accomplish?

She was powerless against whatever was afflicting Chris. And Weston would call if the boy got any worse.

Steeling herself, she took several deep breaths, shut off the engine, then stepped from the car and winced as the Florida heat washed over her.

Squinting against the sun, she slipped the keys into her pocket and looked toward Hoffman's motel room. Her Beretta was in the spare tire well in the rear, and with at least one police officer lingering around the premises, she thought it best to leave it there. One of these days she'd have to figure out a way to land a concealed-carry permit and get the thing on her hip where it belonged.

As she neared Hoffman's door, she noticed it was cracked open. Not surprising. Miller had probably left it open for her.

But as she got closer, she heard someone rummaging around in the room and paused, her gut telling her that something was wrong.

She thought about calling out to Miller, but before she could give it more than that, the door suddenly swung open and she found herself face to face with a tall, thin man with a shaved head and mirrored sunglasses.

She recognized him immediately as the creep sitting on the lip of the fountain outside the courthouse. The guy who'd made her feel like a gazelle in the path of a lion.

She also recognized the battered black satchel in his hand.

It was the judge's.

Before she could say anything, Mr. Sunglasses surged forward and buried his palm hard against her chest. The force knocked her off her feet, slamming her onto the hood of a blue compact car.

The lanky guy didn't hesitate. He turned and took off running.

Swearing under her breath, Kate rolled off the hood of the car and landed on her feet. She spotted the guy angling across the parking lot, long hard strides propelling him away from Kate.

Shit, she thought. I hate foot chases.

But before she could move, she heard someone moaning inside Hoffman's room.

Glancing inside, she saw Detective Miller's body crumpled up on the floor at the foot of the bed. The buzz of a police radio nearby.

She threw one more glance at the fleeing figure, then stepped into the room to help Miller.

•

Kate knelt next to Miller and scanned his injuries.

A gash snaked out from beneath his hairline, stretched down his temple before curling beneath his eye. A glistening trail of blood streamed from the injury, rolling down his cheek and neck before turning the shoulder of his white dress shirt and tan jacket dark. A hand radio lay on the floor a couple feet away from the body.

She could see his chest rising and falling, hear his breath coming in ragged pulls. Uncoiling from the floor, she checked the rest of the room to make sure Mr. Sunglasses hadn't left any friends behind.

She heard a female dispatcher's voice, taut but even, coming from the radio. "Unit thirty-three checkup."

Kate wasn't sure how many times the dispatcher had tried to reach Miller. But she did know if left waiting, the woman would issue an officer-in-distress signal. It would override all the other radio traffic and police would swarm the motel.

"Unit twenty-six to dispatch." Another female.

"Go ahead twenty-six."

"I'm en route to thirty-three's location."

"You're clear, twenty-six." Then she said, "Unit thirty-three checkup."

Kate reached over and picked up Miller's radio, raised it to her mouth and pressed the transmit button.

"Detective Miller's injured," she said. "I'm here with him. He's in room six, but he needs first aid and an ambulance."

"Identify."

"Kate Messenger," she said, then hesitated. "I'm from another jurisdiction. Trying to help him. Repeat. He needs first aid and an ambulance. He's been hit in the head and he's bleeding."

By now, she was in the bathroom, plucking dingy white towels from a wire wall rack.

Kate heard sirens growing louder outside the motel. When she exited the bathroom, she heard the roar of a patrol car and the thump as it rolled from the street into the parking lot.

The female cop's voice cut in. "Twenty-six to dispatch. I'm on scene with unit twelve."

"You're clear twenty-six."

Kate tossed the radio onto the bed. She knelt next to Miller and pressed the towel against the cut. She guessed it was the cleanest thing in the room, which wasn't saying much.

A petite woman, her torso made boxy by a tactical vest, rolled through the door, her pistol gripped with both hands.

She leveled the muzzle at Kate and ordered her to stand.

Kate left the towel on Miller's head, then rose to her feet and held up her hands.

20

KATE SPENT THE NEXT HOUR at the motel.

The officer who had ordered her to her feet quickly saw that she'd been trying to help Miller, and by the time the paramedics arrived, Miller was conscious and seated on the edge of the bed.

With two fingers, he had gingerly probed the spot on his head where he'd been struck, wincing each time he touched the wound.

Kate had been watching him for awhile and, even when not poking at his wound, he looked miserable—and she knew why. After knocking Miller unconscious, Mr. Sunglasses had also lifted his gun and badge. And Miller would undoubtedly catch hell for this in equal measures from his superiors and colleagues.

Once the paramedics finished with him, Kate threaded her

way through the room until she was standing next to him. "How's the head?"

"Still attached." He flashed a weak smile. "That should count for something."

"Especially in our line of work."

The officer who had been the first on the scene strode toward them. Kate noted the captain's bars on her shoulders and her confident gait.

Kate pegged her at five feet, four inches, and less than a hundred and twenty pounds, minus her ballistic vest and gun belt. She was slim and pretty, with full lips and pale blue eyes. Her blonde hair was cut in a pixie. Her skin was tanned deep brown. There were small lines around at the corners of her eyes and Kate guessed they were about the same age.

She looked at Miller. "You doing okay, Arlan?"

"Define 'okay', Cap. I'm alive." He nodded at Kate. "Probably because she showed up when she did."

The woman turned to Kate. "You're Kate Messenger, right? I heard you on the radio." She offered a hand to shake. "Melanie Tanner."

Kate shook her hand.

"The man who hit the detective," Tanner said. "You saw him?"

Kate nodded. "Briefly. I was outside when I heard a noise. I walked up to the door. It flew open. This guy blew past me."

Tanner, who had pulled a small notepad and a silver pen from her shirt pocket, nodded and made an encouraging sound as she scribbled down notes.

"What did he look like?"

"Tall. Shaved head. Very thin. Sunglasses." Kate pieced together a vague clothing description. "He went by fast, knocked me out of the way. Before I could chase him—"

Tanner stopped writing and looked up at Kate. "Hold up. Chase him? Why would you chase him?"

"I used to be on the job."

"Here in Florida?"

"California."

Nodding, Tanner scribbled in her notebook again. "Are you staying at this motel? Is that why you're here?"

"She's just visiting," Miller said. "She knew Hoffman."

Tanner gave a curt nod. "Sorry. Was he a friend?"

"More of a professional acquaintance," Kate said.

Something flickered in the other woman's eyes. "Did you come here with him?"

"No. We didn't know each other that well."

"But you were in Florida at the same time as him."

Kate nodded. "I saw a news report about his DUI arrest. I came down here," she paused, "to see if I could help him."

"All the way from California?"

"I was visiting friends in Alabama."

"I see," Tanner said. "And when did you first learn about his murder?"

"That was from me," Miller said. "I called her out to the scene early this morning to ask her some questions."

She nodded and looked at Kate. "So why were you here at the motel?"

Kate and Miller exchanged a brief glance and she could see that her answer could get him in hot water, but before she could speak, her phone vibrated in her hand.

Her stomach fluttered when she saw the number of Weston's pay-as-you-go cell phone flashing on the screen. Earlier, while the paramedics attended to Miller, she had texted Weston twice and was told that nothing with Chris had changed.

Now she feared the worst.

She held up her phone to Tanner, her voice a little hoarse. "Mind if I take this?"

"Go ahead."

Tanner pocketed her notebook and pen, then turned and walked over to a small knot of cops and started talking to them.

Kate drifted away from Miller and stepped outside as she brought the phone to her ear and flicked it on. "Please tell me this is good news."

"It is," Weston said. "He's awake, tired as hell, and still a little cold, but he's warmed up considerably."

"Oh, thank God." A wave of relief washed over Kate. "Is he communicating yet?"

"No, but the worst part seems over. I guess he knows himself better than we do."

"I'm still worried he's holding out on us. This whole Jennifer thing has me spooked."

"You and me both," Weston said, then paused. "What's going on over there? What's all that noise?"

"Things got complicated."

"In what way?"

She relayed the events of the last hour, including Miller getting hit on the head, and Mr. Sunglasses knocking her onto the hood of the car.

"Christ," Weston said. "And you're sure this is the guy you saw at the courthouse during Hoffman's arraignment?"

"Yes."

"Interesting. What did he steal?"

"Miller's gun and badge," Kate said. "And a satchel. The same satchel Hoffman was hanging onto yesterday like it was a precious artifact. So, whatever's in it must be worth something." She paused, unable to get the boy off her mind. "Are you sure Chris is okay? I hate it when he doesn't communicate."

"Don't worry, he's fine. He'll open up eventually."

She sighed. "Okay, good, because I have a feeling I'll be here awhile longer."

They said goodbye and Kate ended the call. As she pocketed her phone, Miller stepped outside and joined her.

He massaged the back of his head with one hand, and extended the other to Kate. "Thank you. I might be dead if it weren't for you."

Kate acknowledged him with a tight smile and a nod. "The guy who hit you, he was carrying a small satchel. Any idea what was in it?"

"Not a clue. He clocked me as soon as I walked through the door."

Kate nodded. "I thought that was probably how it went down. Looks like he did a pretty thorough search of the room. Mattress sliced open, drawers pulled out."

"Not that there was much reason for it. The old man traveled light and didn't unpack his suitcase. Guy sliced open the lining, too. You think that satchel was what he was after? Or did it belong to him?"

Kate kept what she knew to herself. "I was too busy getting knocked down to ask. Did you search the judge's car?"

"If we had, I probably wouldn't be able to tell you. But we didn't find crap, so what the hell? Fast food bags wadded up and stuffed under the seats. Some empty liquor bottles. Bullshit, mostly." He paused. "Hey, listen to me, spilling my guts…"

Kate served up what she hoped was her most disarming smile. "I'm good people, remember? Besides, I have that kind of face."

He smirked at her. "Sure, that must be it. Or maybe it's the hit on the gourd. Whatever. My head's on fire."

"Will you be okay? Do you need a ride somewhere?"

"Nah, paramedics say I'm fine to drive. I'll just go home, douse the fire with a few nips of scotch. Maybe take an aspirin or two along the way. Sleep it off. Not the first time I've taken a hit to the head." He gestured toward Hoffman's room. "Not sure whether you were planning on leaving any time soon, but you'd better check with the captain. Make sure she doesn't have any more questions. You do not want to piss that woman off."

"Thanks for the advice," Kate said.

"And I'd appreciate it if you left out the part about me inviting you here. I didn't tell her anything about the little ruse you pulled yesterday."

"I have no idea what you're talking about."

He smiled and gave her a thumbs-up, then turned and headed up the sidewalk toward a cluster of white Ford sedans, keys jingling in his hand. He hadn't walked more than a few yards before he halted and turned back to Kate. "Hey, do you know a Barbara Adams?"

Kate shook her head. "Means nothing to me. Why?"

"Ah, don't worry about it."

"Bullshit."

Miller grinned. "All right. We found her name written on a piece of paper in Hoffman's car. I thought maybe she was somebody he knew in Santa Flora."

Kate shrugged. "I can make some calls if you want."

He waved her off. "Don't worry about it. Much as I like talking to you, I think maybe it's time for you to wish your friend a happy life in eternity and move along."

"Maybe," she said. "Now go home and take some aspirin."

She stared after him as he ambled to his car and climbed inside.

She felt unsettled. She'd had a good feeling about Miller from the start, but now she was wondering why he was being so open and accepting of Weston and her. Even flattering her a bit. Was it simply because she may have saved his life?

If the roles were reversed, and she had a murder to solve, she'd be looking at this the way the Feds were, with more than a passing curiosity in a woman from the victim's home-town who'd shown up just before the killing. Especially one traveling with an alleged mass murderer.

Maybe Miller was sincere. Maybe he *did* know people, as he'd told them at the crime scene. And he certainly had a couple dozen IQ points over Page and Jefferson.

So, was he playing it sly? Did he have his own agenda?

Kate shook her head, her thoughts racing a million miles an hour, always coming back to the name he had just men-tioned.

Barbara Adams.

She hadn't lied about that. It meant nothing to her.

So, who was this woman?

Contrary to Miller's advice, Kate got on her phone and fired off a text message to Matt Nava at Santa Flora PD, asking him to look into the name and see if she had any ties to Judge John Hoffman.

Thirty seconds later, her phone pinged.

You're kidding right? You do realize I have a job here? If MacLean catches me freelancing on work computers, it'll be my ass.

Kate typed a reply:

Never use "MacLean" and "ass" in the same sentence. It's redundant.

The phone pinged again several seconds later.

Translation: "You don't care." Understood. Let me start running some traps.

Grinning, Kate stowed the phone in her purse.

21

WHEN SHE RETURNED TO THEIR motel, Kate found
Christopher still in bed and Weston napping in a chair next to
it.

She put a hand on Chris's forehead, relieved to find his
temperature back to normal, then decided to use the time to
run down a couple of leads she hadn't passed along to Nava.

For starters, she wanted to know more about Hoffman's
attorney.

Angela Lowenthal.

She got on her phone, ran the name through a search
engine and got several hits. Lowenthal was older than she
looked, flirting with forty, but looking ten years younger.
Whether it was good genetics or a good plastic surgeon was
anyone's guess.

She had attended law school in Orlando. When she graduated, she worked for the district attorney's office before joining a law firm there—Richelson, Taylor and Ward.

The firm was small but well-established. It had two offices in Florida—Orlando and Tallahassee—and one in Washington, D.C. According to a couple of news articles, it was retained primarily by Florida's old money families.

Kate's brow furrowed. Hoffman wasn't destitute—at least she didn't think he was—but he also wasn't from old money.

He'd told Kate on more than one occasion he'd grown up the son of working class parents. He'd joined the military to pay for college, had liked it well enough to serve two hitches while attending night school. He'd left the Marines and, with his new wife, had returned to California where he'd attended UCLA law school before moving to Santa Flora.

As Kate thought about it, she recalled some campaign-season whispers around the department about Hoffman's finances. When news surfaced that he and his wife owned a few rental properties in suburban Los Angeles, people began to question where a judge—a public employee—had gotten the cash. There were insinuations that he'd received the money from criminals in exchange for favorable treatment.

Before it ballooned into a full-out scandal, however, his wife Eva had held a press conference announcing that the money had been a gift from her family, and the heat around the matter quickly dissipated.

Kate knew very little about Hoffman's wife. Eva had always seemed like the stereotypical political accessory. She was pretty, but not so much that she sucked attention away from her husband. She did a lot of holding onto Hoffman's arm and gazing at him adoringly as he spoke. Hoffman had loved the woman, no question about it, but Kate viewed Eva as a Stepford wife, lovely yet empty. Well trained in a finishing school sort of way.

width:951px; height:1519px;

The kind of training that comes from money.

So, if Hoffman still had ties to his in-laws, having an expensive attorney might make sense.

But he wasn't involved with the family.

At least that was the story he'd told people.

But Kate was starting to wonder whether it was true.

She sighed, navigated away from the search screen, then called Lowenthal's number and left a brief message on her voicemail. She mentioned knowing the judge through her work at the police department, inferring that she still was a detective without actually saying it. A lie by omission.

The way Kate saw it, the attorney wouldn't be anxious to discuss a client with anyone. But if she believed Kate still was a police officer, she might at least feel obligated to return the call, even if she declined to say anything.

Might.

Miller himself had said he couldn't get in touch with her.

Kate shifted back to the search engine to hunt for information about Eva Hoffman and her family. She started by digging up a couple of profiles of the judge from the Santa Flora newspapers.

About halfway through the second article, she found Eva's maiden name—Prescott—and a mention of the kids, but little else.

With a little more searching, she found an obituary that mentioned a surviving daughter: Eva Prescott Hoffman.

Bingo.

The dead man was William Prescott III, the retired chairman of a Tallahassee-based communications firm. The obit was an article that had run on the Associated Press wire service and picked up by the *Santa Flora Star*. Kate wasn't a journalist, but she knew enough to understand that not everyone rated an obituary written by an wire-service reporter.

William Prescott—at least in some circles—was a big deal.

Kate read the first few paragraphs of the obit. Prescott was the third generation owner of Prescott Communications, a chain of newspapers and television stations spread throughout the southern U.S.

He had also been a decorated Army officer during the Korean War and later in life had sat on the boards of several community organizations—abuse shelters, group homes, soup kitchens—and a couple of newspaper trade groups.

There were a lot of glowing quotes from his peers in the media industry. His family obviously had amassed power and wealth, but Kate saw no hints of controversy about his life.

Just a standard, run-of-the-mill billionaire.

She was about to run her own on check on Barbara Adams, the name Miller had mentioned, when she heard Weston stirring in the other room.

She pocketed her phone, stepped through the adjoining doorway and found him stretching and yawning.

She gestured to Chris. "I think his temperature's back to normal."

Noah nodded. "But he's hardly moved. I've never seen him out this long."

"What do you make of it?" she asked.

He nodded in the direction of her room, then stepped past her and went through the doorway. Kate followed, then pushed the door closed and leaned against it, crossing her arms over her chest.

"Okay, what's up?"

"Someone's playing a game with us."

Kate frowned. "You mean Chris?"

"No," he said, and she detected an undercurrent of fear in

his tone. "I don't always understand the boy or how he operates. But he wouldn't screw with us like this. What we're doing is too important to him."

"Then what do you think is going on?"

"It's exactly what you asked him about before you left for Hoffman's place. I think the one playing games is the girl in that picture I drew."

"Jennifer."

Weston nodded. "After we got off the phone, Chris started communicating with me, but he seemed to have difficulty doing it and he didn't go into much detail. But what he *did* say was that his little conversations with her had come uninvited. And against his will."

Kate felt a chill.

Weston went on. "We both know these episodes are anything but normal. Which leads me to wonder if he hasn't been able to go to his usual happy place, because Jennifer won't let him. This isn't like what he has with Lucy. She's not just communicating with him sporadically, and I doubt she's all that friendly. She's inside his head and it's all her all the time. And she's getting stronger."

Kate balked. "That's seems like a pretty big leap."

"Think about it. You said you thought Jennifer was the one who made you black out. What if she's doing everything she can to block Chris from communicating with anyone else, and that's why he keeps shutting down?"

"Okay, but why would she do that?"

"I don't know. Maybe she's been wanting someone to listen to her for a long time, and now that she's found him, she won't let him go."

Kate thought about this. "Didn't Chris say that he and Lucy had to be within a certain range for them to talk? What if we take him out of the city? If what you're suggesting is true, eventually Jennifer will lose her grip on him."

"You're assuming she's landlocked. We don't know that. For all we know, she'll pull up a chair inside his head and ride along with him. We may never be rid of her."

"Jesus. If she's some kind of spirit or whatever, can't he just block her or kick her out of his head or whatever it is he does?"

"Judging by the way he's been acting and what he told me, it doesn't seem like it. And unless he can get away from her, break her hold over his mind, he won't be able to pick up other signals."

"This is crazy," she said.

"That's sort of our thing, isn't it?"

Kate felt sick. If this had been a conventional crime, she would've known how to handle it. She hadn't spent a lot of time around children, but if she could find a way to speak with the little girl, maybe that would make a difference.

Maybe.

But if what Weston was saying had any truth to it at all, how could she communicate with a spirit or whatever the hell this girl was? Especially one who was able to shut her down in seconds flat.

The answer was easy. She couldn't.

Not unless the spirit decided to speak with *her*.

And whether that would happen was anyone's guess.

PART TWO

"Children are the anchors that hold a mother to life."

~Sophocles

22

THE LAW OFFICES OF RICHELSON, Taylor and Ward were located on the 18th floor of a sleek tower of smoky black glass.

Kate sat scanning the building's lobby as well-dressed office workers streamed in through the front doors. She was waiting for Angela Lowenthal, the judge's attorney, to arrive.

Earlier, when Kate had awoken, she'd found Christopher up and dressed. His bed was made and he was sitting in a chair.

Weston told her the boy had awakened in the middle of the night, changed clothes and devoured several pieces of fruit and a granola bar. He had ignored Weston's questions before moving into his trancelike haze, and had been that way ever since.

Although they were both racked with concern, Weston had again decided he would stay behind with the boy while Kate found out what she could about Hoffman. And since Lowenthal hadn't yet bothered to return Kate's call, they figured a face-to-face was in order.

Kate had been in the building less than fifteen minutes when Lowenthal streamed in with the crowd—red suit, phone pressed to her ear, briefcase clutched in her other hand.

Her gait was quick and direct. Passing a pair of old men in suits, she greeted them with a smile and waggled the fingers of her phone hand in a wave, never slowing her pace. Kate guessed the woman lived at a dead run.

She got up from her chair, hurried past the old men and fell in behind Lowenthal, trailing her and several others into the elevator. By the time they reached the 18th floor, Lowenthal had finished her call and was stowing her phone as the doors parted.

Kate stepped from the elevator first, paused and reached into her purse as though searching for something.

Once the other woman brushed past her, Kate raised her eyes from her purse. "Ms. Lowenthal?"

The other woman paused and turned toward Kate. "Yes?"

"You're John Hoffman's attorney, right?"

Lowenthal's brow furrowed. "And you are?"

"Kate Messenger. We met briefly at the courthouse. After his arraignment."

Lowenthal paused for a second before recognition dawned. She gave Kate a curt nod and a cool smile. "I remember you. John told me you knew him from California. Horrible thing that happened to him."

"Very much so."

"Can I help you with something?"

"I'd like a few minutes to speak with you."

Lowenthal glanced at her watch. "About?"

"John."

"I gathered that much. Can you be a little more specific?"

"About how he died," Kate said.

Lowenthal sighed. "Ms. Messenger. John told me you used to be a police officer. I'm sure you can understand that, as his attorney, I can't say anything about him. Attorney-client privilege doesn't expire just because the client is dead."

"I know that."

"Then you probably also know that his passing—"

"Murder," Kate said.

Lowenthal worked her mouth for a moment without emitting a sound. "Yes, his murder. While unfortunate, it also means that the state will drop the criminal charges against him, and I need to start working on making that happen. So if you'll excuse me..."

Lowenthal spun toward her office suite and started away.

"Counselor, did the Prescotts hire you to represent John?"

Lowenthal jerked to a halt and turned, glaring at Kate.

"That," she said, "is none of your business."

Kate knew this woman would never tell her a damn thing, but something tingled inside her brain. A sudden thought that made no rational sense when it came to John Hoffman, yet there it was, and she let it out without hesitating.

"Jennifer thinks it's our business."

Lowenthal blinked at her, as if she'd just been slapped across the face.

Then she looked away. "This conversation is over. Get out. If you're still here in five minutes, I'll have you thrown out."

She turned abruptly, moving toward her office, Kate knowing she'd struck a chord and wondering how she had even managed it.

What possible connection could the angry little girl who

was playing with Christopher's mind have with Judge Hoffman?

But then Jennifer's sudden appearance in their life *did* seem awfully convenient.

Was she here because of John?

•

Kate rode the elevator to the first floor.

When she stepped into the lobby, two men—both dressed in khakis and blue shirts with button-down collars—were positioned outside the bank of elevators. Kate recognized the taller of the two as the white-haired military man she'd seen trailing behind Hoffman and Lowenthal at the courthouse.

She was about to turn toward the lobby doors and head out, so maybe they'd see her leaving and back off. But she doubted it.

They looked like they wanted to make a point.

The taller man rushed up on Kate, stopping inches away from her. Thick through the arms and shoulders, he reeked of an ashtray doused in cologne, the smell accented by traces of last night's beer binge. Up close, she noticed his hair had been yellowed by cigarette smoke.

He crossed his thick arms over his chest. "Time for you to go."

She smirked. "The way I figure it, I still have a good three minutes left." She held up her hands. "But don't worry, big guy. I'm not here to cause trouble."

She turned and headed for the exit, the goon squad a step behind her. When she pushed through the lobby doors, they didn't follow.

But they were watching her.

She could feel their gazes burning into her back.

Funny, but they didn't strike her as the type of goons a white shoe law firm or a luxury office building would hire.

They seemed more like the kind of hired muscle a crime boss would surround himself with.

So what did that mean? And why had mentioning Chris's uninvited friend to Lowenthal made such an impact?

Her mind racing, Kate reached the sidewalk and started for the Rambler, which was parked down the street.

Someone behind her said, "So the Gestapo got you, too, huh?"

She recognized the voice and stopped in her tracks.

Cindy Davis.

Wow, this morning just kept getting better.

Turning, she found Davis standing a couple feet away, dressed in another expensive suit, a nervous expression fixed on her face.

"Why the hell are you following me?" Kate asked.

"Following you? Really?"

"Cop stalking is your MO."

Davis scowled. "I don't *stalk* cops. I have sources."

"I'm not one of them."

"Yeah, no kidding. You're an unemployed troublemaker. What makes you think I need anything from you?"

"You're not making me like you any better."

Davis gave her a look. "Like me? I thought that ship had already sailed." Then, surprisingly, she softened a bit. "Listen, Kate, I've been wanting to tell you this for a long time, but I just didn't have the nerve. I'm sorry about the stuff I wrote about your mother. The source seemed good. I went with what I had and it was wrong."

"I could've told you that."

"You did." She showed a weak smile. "You also threw in a few unflattering things about my own ancestry. I don't blame you. I would've done the same thing. Tell me you've never fallen for a bad tip."

"When I get a bad tip," Kate said, "I don't publish it for thousands of people to see."

Davis sighed. "Look, I'm sure we could do this all day, but I said what I wanted to say. If you want to stay pissed at me, be my guest." She looked at her watch. "I've gotta go, but I'm glad I ran into you again."

Kate held up a hand for her to stop. Something other than the apology was nagging at her. "So those goons booted you out, too?"

Davis nodded. "They did."

Kate swallowed hard. She couldn't believe she was about to say this. "Do you have time for a cup of coffee?"

"Why? So you can throw it in my face?"

"And waste good coffee?"

Davis laughed. "Well, well, the lady has a sense of humor after all."

"Is that yes or no?"

Davis glanced at her watch again, then gestured. "Lead the way."

23

THEY FOUND A FAST FOOD PLACE down the street.

Kate ordered coffee and an English muffin stuffed with a sausage patty, a cheese slice, and a yellow thing that looked like a hockey puck cut in half that she assumed was an egg. Davis bought a bottle of water, a cup of tea, and an egg white on a low-calorie English muffin. She separated the egg white and the bread and picked at the egg with her fork.

Kate nodded at Davis's food. "I thought reporters ate crap."

"I still do. But I have a book coming out next month. That means lots of television interviews. Some book signings. My agent wants me thin. Sort of turns my stomach playing that game, but I like the royalty checks."

"Another true crime book?"

Davis nodded. "Murder in a small town in Nevada. An

entire family—the Sheltons—was killed. Horrible stuff. My agent says it'll be the next *In Cold Blood*."

Kate was biting into her sandwich when she paused. These murders sounded all too familiar. "They ever catch the killer?"

Davis shook her head. "Whoever it was, was a psycho. He butchered that poor family. Beat and stabbed them. Stole their truck and their money before he disappeared."

Kate covered her mouth with her napkin. "Any suspects?"

She nodded. "They had a ranch. When they got busy, they'd hire a drifter or two to work there. Not the smartest move in the world, if you ask me, but to each his own. Apparently, they'd hired a guy a week or so before."

Kate's skin prickled and a feeling of dread washed over her.

"Like I said," Davis continued, "he was only there for a few days so the neighbors never got to know him. They didn't remember much about him, except that he was big. He kept his hair clipped down to stubble. Vance Shelton—that was the father—told a neighbor the guy was just passing through Nevada. He'd been stationed at a naval base in California, had been discharged, and was heading back east. He'd run out of money. The Sheltons loved to pick up strays and they gave him a job."

Kate's gut was churning. She set down her food and pushed it away.

Davis looked at her. "Are you all right?"

Kate nodded. "It's just a shame they never solved it."

Davis shrugged. "I doubt they ever will. That was 1995. There wasn't a lot of information about the guy. Shelton paid people under the table, so there were no tax forms or check stubs. The guy was in and gone before anyone even realized the family had been killed. They had his first name—Mickey

—and that was it."

Kate swallowed hard. "Mickey?"

"Like the mouse. I know. Not very menacing, is it?"

Kate sat back in her seat. Michael Bonner—the mall security guard who had murdered her mother, the man she'd come to know as the Beast—had also been known as Mickey. Kate wasn't sure whether it was his real name or an alias, and running it through search engines and police databases had gotten her nowhere. Shortly after her mother's murder, Bonner had quit his job at the mall and disappeared. It was possible he'd fled California by way of Nevada.

A million questions swirled through her mind.

"Are you sure you're okay?" Davis asked. "You look like you've seen a—"

"Did they ever pick up this guy's trail again?"

Davis shook her head. "Pretty hard to do when you don't have a photo, a last name, or any other identifying information."

No kidding, Kate thought. Even a last name hadn't helped.

"So now that we're best buds and all," Davis said. "Tell me something."

"Don't get ahead of yourself."

"I'm just curious. How did you end up on a road trip with this guy Noah Weston?"

Kate visibly stiffened and Davis raised her hands to reassure her.

"This isn't a trick," she said. "It's completely off the record. I promise. Really."

"And I trust you about as far as I can throw you."

Davis nodded. "Okay, I get that. I don't blame you. But, really, it's just an innocent question. I mean, he seems a little grim for my taste, but he isn't hard to look at."

"It isn't like that."

"Then what's it like?"

"Why don't you ask Bob MacLean," Kate said.

"I did. He said you took Weston into custody a while back and interrogated him about a murder, but he was cleared of it. MacLean didn't know much more than that."

Kate nodded. When she'd interrogated Weston, she'd been too pissed at MacLean to discuss it with him. Or anyone else for that matter.

"There wasn't much more to know," Kate said.

Davis stared at her, apparently expecting her to continue. Instead, Kate sat still, her hands resting one on top of the other, staring right back.

It wasn't even a minute before Davis began shifting in her chair. "Come on, Kate, throw me a bone, here. I told you, I'm just curious. What's going on between you two?"

"Nothing romantic, if that's what you're getting at."

Davis shook her head. "No, not romantic. But you've both been through the same thing."

Kate felt herself stiffen again. She thought about Page and Jefferson's accusations and knew she was treading on dangerous ground.

"Really?" she said. "Enlighten me."

"You both lost people close to you. Your mother's murder went unsolved. And assuming Weston's innocent—"

"He is."

"—then his family's murder is unsolved, right?"

Kate nodded, then Davis said something unexpected.

"So you're trying to help him solve it. Maybe make up for your mom's case going cold." She leaned back in her seat, spread her hands and smiled. "Did I nail it?"

Kate frowned. "Why are you even asking me about this?"

"I have my reasons."

"Right," Kate said, "because you're a coroner-chasing

ghoul who gets off on other people's suffering."

Davis's brow suddenly furrowed and Kate knew that she'd just hit a sore spot.

Davis stared into her tea, which she held in both hands. "You don't know much about me, do you?"

And never wanted to, Kate thought.

"Not really, no."

"I'm not a ghoul, okay? That's not what I am."

Davis paused and looked at Kate. Her eyes were moist and she seemed to be asking for something with her gaze.

Then she said, "I know what it's like to lose someone. When I was a girl, my older brother disappeared for several days. Even though he was only sixteen, that wasn't entirely unusual for him. He was angry. He drank a lot, got into fights. Had run-ins with the local police."

She paused and set her cup down.

"Sometimes he'd take up with an older woman. He'd stay a few days, usually until she found out he was underage or saw how violent and lazy he was. He'd get thrown out and come back home, and my parents were always glad to see him."

She looked at Kate.

"I get that. He was their son, right? But then one time, a week before Thanksgiving, he snuck out of the house after my parents went to bed. I caught him, asked him where he was going and he balled up his fist, showed it to me and told me to go back to bed. Threatened to hit me if I didn't listen to him. He'd hit me before—a lot—so I knew he meant it."

Shuddering, her gaze fell to the table, eyes glistening with tears.

"Anyway, when he didn't come home, my parents didn't think anything of it for a couple of days. He'd dropped out of school, had no job, so it wasn't like anybody else cared, either. We'd been through this so many times before, it was normal."

She paused, cleared her throat and sipped from her tea.

"On the fourth day, a policeman came to the house. I answered the door and he asked to speak with my mom or dad. He looked really uncomfortable and I knew something bad had happened. When you grow up like that, you know when something bad's coming. So I found my mother..."

Her throat had grown hoarse. She paused and swallowed hard.

"Long story short, someone had murdered my brother. They'd beaten him and dumped his body in a cornfield. They never found the killer. That was thirty-three years ago. Whoever killed him is probably dead and gone by now. But there isn't a day where I don't think about it, wonder if I had told my parents he was leaving, that maybe he'd be alive."

Davis looked at her again and Kate acknowledged her words with a nod.

"I'm sorry," Kate said, and she really meant it.

Davis shrugged. "Ever since then, I've been pretty much obsessed with murder. Like this Harbinger thing. I always think if I put the information out there, maybe it'll help someone, but so far my track record's pretty shitty. I've reported on dozens of cases and most of them are still unsolved."

"You can only do so much," Kate said.

Davis nodded, picked up her napkin, and dabbed at the corners of her eyes. She glanced at her watch and muttered a curse. "Hey, I really do have to get going."

Turning in her seat, she rummaged through her purse, found a business card and slid it across the table at Kate.

"I meant what I said about being sorry. I hope you believe me."

For the first time, Kate did and she nodded.

"Anyway, if I can ever help you two in anyway, give me a call. I'll keep it all strictly off the record unless you want me to do otherwise. I don't normally do that."

Kate took the card and figured this was a good time to get to the real reason she'd invited Davis for coffee.

"Maybe you can help me right now," she said.

"Okay. What?"

"One of those guys on the goon squad. The white-haired guy? Looks ex-military. I saw him at the courthouse tagging along with Lowenthal and Judge Hoffman. You know anything about him?"

"Yeah," Davis said. "He's bad news."

"What do you mean?"

"His name's Jack Baker. He's a professional thug. He dresses in expensive suits, drives a BMW ragtop, and lives in a nice neighborhood. But he's a thug. A fixer, really."

"What does he fix?"

"Rumor has it he does the firm's less than legal work. If they can't get a document legally, he's the guy who bribes or blackmails someone into giving it up. If they want to pay off a witness, he's the guy delivering the money."

"Is he violent?"

"You've met him," Davis said. "You tell me."

"What's his background?"

"I don't know. I haven't looked too far into it. What little I do, I learned secondhand and I'm putting Lowenthal down as a 'declined comment' on any future stories. It'll save me a lot of trouble."

"So what do you plan to write about John?"

"I'm not sure. But now I think he's just a sad little side note in this Harbinger thing. Maybe another victim, maybe not. Between us, I feel sorry for the guy. He seemed like a lonely old man with a drinking problem. And I guess in a way he was like you and me and your friend Weston. He lost people who were close to him, only he never recovered."

Kate said nothing, but thought maybe she and Weston hadn't either.

"Speaking of which," Davis said. "Did you hear about what happened last night?"

"No, what?"

"They found another dead woman. They think the Harbinger did it."

24

"THAT'S WHERE THEY FOUND THE body," Kate said.

She tapped a finger against the Rambler's windshield, pointing at a small clapboard row house, the white paint bubbling and peeling. The house was on a corner and police had put up yellow tape around the perimeter. A half dozen cruisers and unmarked cars surrounded the property and officers milled around the yard or stood in the driveway or street.

After hearing the news, Kate had driven back to the motel, picked up Weston and Chris, and let Weston drive as she navigated.

Weston parked the Rambler along a curb, behind a news van, and let the vehicle idle, the air conditioner blasting cool air onto their faces. Kate turned around in her seat and looked at Christopher. The boy was squeezing his eyes shut. Deep creases lined his forehead. His jaw worked, clenching and unclenching, and frustration radiated from him.

She glanced at Weston and saw concern etched on his features.

I'm not getting anything, Chris said.

He looked at Kate now, his gaze fixed on her, an intensity radiating from him. Kate sensed it, felt it surround her like a fourth presence in the vehicle.

I don't feel anything. Nothing!

"It's okay," Kate said.

He shook his head.

Why is she doing this to me? I don't understand it!

He sounded young, frustrated, like a boy in way over his head. And, without his abilities, that's exactly what he was.

Weston said, "Don't worry son. We'll figure this out." He turned to Kate. "You go to the scene. I'll wait here with him."

Kate nodded.

Gathering up her purse, she exited the Rambler and headed for the house. A crowd had formed outside the police barricades. Kate assumed it was mostly neighbors.

A TV news reporter was interviewing a young woman clad in a T-shirt, cutoff denim shorts, and sandals. The woman had a baby cradled in her arms, its face buried against her breast as she swayed soothingly and spoke to a young reporter.

Kate nearly rolled her eyes, figuring they were doing the requisite "terrified neighbor" interview.

As she neared the house, she scanned the crowd, looking for any familiar faces, thinking about Mr. Sunglasses.

What she'd stumbled into at Hoffman's motel room could have been nothing more than a random burglary, but then why had he been hanging around outside the courthouse? And what random burglar steals a battered old satchel?

Could *he* have had something to do with this? And with

John's murder as well?

Too many questions and not enough answers.

She pushed her way through the crowd until she reached a barricade manned by a police officer in shorts, mirrored sunglasses and a bicycle helmet, his thumbs hooked over the edges of his belt. He appeared to be watching the crowd, though it was hard to tell for sure with his eyes hidden.

"I'm here to see Detective Miller," she said.

"He's busy, ma'am."

"I'm sure he is."

The guy fell silent. He probably figured if he ignored Kate long enough, she'd go away. She'd used the same technique more times than she cared to count and it had usually worked for her.

"My name's Kate Messenger. I've been consulting with Miller on this case."

The bicycle officer smirked. "Yeah? Which paper do you work for?"

Kate kept her expression stony. "Call Detective Miller and tell him I want to see him."

"Ma'am he has more important—"

"It's okay, John," Miller said.

Kate looked past the cop's shoulder and saw Miller approaching. His polo shirt was dark with sweat, plastered against his skin. "Come in, Kate."

Nodding, she squeezed between two of the sawhorse barricades.

As they walked toward the house, Miller said, "I thought you folks were heading out."

Kate shrugged. "I heard the news and thought I'd swing by." She gestured. "What do you have in there?"

"A young woman. We don't have a positive ID yet. Possibly a hooker. Or sex worker or whatever we're supposed to call them now. Judging by the scene, she wasn't killed here. I'm guessing there were a dozen stab wounds to the face, neck and torso, but no evidence that she actually bled here. No defensive wounds on the hands or forearms. Rope marks on the wrists and ankles, so she couldn't move."

"She was killed somewhere else and brought here."

"Yeah. If she fits the mold with the others, she was held somewhere for a few days before she was killed. I'm guessing she was sexually assaulted, too. Forensics is inside right now. That's why I'm out here, so I don't contaminate the scene. There's some blood on the walls, so they can collect that, maybe get something."

"I thought you said she didn't bleed here."

"She didn't. But there was blood. The crazy bastard drew another circle with a dot in the center on one of the walls of the room where he strung her up. This time it looks like he used blood. We're assuming it belongs to the victim, but we won't know that until we get the lab results back. Looks like he used his hand to spread the blood around. We're hoping we can find some fingerprints."

Kate's stomach lurched.

"You look a little pale," Miller said. "You need to sit down?"

"I'm fine," she told him. "So he used spray paint last time. This time, he uses blood."

"And he never drew these symbols until recently. What do you think?"

"I think he's escalating."

Miller nodded. "I think you're right. And there's one thing that symbol confirms in my book."

"What's that?"

"That the Harbinger may be back to his usual choice of victims now, but the judge was definitely one of them. I'm thinking my theory was right. He got wind that the task force thought Hoffman was their man and he figured he'd send a message. Then he does this just to rub their noses in it."

Contrary to her earlier belief, Kate was beginning to think he might be right about John being a victim of the Harbinger, but the motive still felt wrong. There had to another reason John was killed.

But what was it?

And why had he even come to Apalache Springs?

And, most importantly, how the hell did this entity who was plaguing Christopher fit into the picture? Why had the mention of Jennifer's name gotten such a strong reaction from Angela Lowenthal?

Too many questions.

Not enough goddamn answers.

"Forced entry?" she asked Miller.

"No signs of that," he said. "Not sure it was necessary. All the doors were unlocked when the uniforms found the body."

Kate mulled that over. The killer had to know these homes were vacant. Not that it took a ton of guesswork to figure it out.

Like the house that Hoffman was found in, the mailbox was stuffed full. Flyers for local businesses littered the front porch. Still, bringing bodies into the homes and arranging the crime scenes required time. It wasn't like dumping a corpse into a ravine and speeding off in the car.

Kate guessed the killer knew the neighborhood and the property. Or *killers*, if Christopher had been right the other night—although his reliability at the moment was iffy.

Whoever did this may have watched the house for a few days to make sure it was vacant. Or had even toured it as a potential tenant.

"Do you know who owns the property?" Kate asked.

Miller shook his head. "But I should pretty soon."

25

JUST AS KATE, WESTON AND CHRIS pulled into the parking lot of their motel, Kate's phone rang.

Picking it up, she saw the Santa Flora PD's general number flashing on her screen and hoped it was Matt Nava with news about the name the cops had found on that scrap of paper in John's Caddie.

She brought the Rambler to a stop near their door and turned to Weston. "Why don't you get Chris inside. I need to take this."

Weston nodded and as he hustled Chris out of the car, Kate tapped the talk button and brought the phone to her ear. "Kate Messenger."

"Hey," Nava said.

"Hey yourself. You come up with anything on our friend Barbara? Because I sure as hell couldn't."

The air conditioner was working decently for a change, so she let the Rambler idle for a second.

"What's that noise?" Nava asked. "Are you in a biplane?"

"I'm in a... never mind." Killing the engine, she rolled down a window and immediately wished she hadn't. The humidity was stifling. "Tell me you've got good news."

"If by good you mean did I find a woman who should've been impossible to locate with a name as common as hers? Then, yeah. I don't know what Barbara Adams's deal is, but she's way off the grid. A lesser man would've thrown in the towel."

"I knew I could count on you," Kate said. "What'd you learn?"

"Barbara Adams. Maiden name was Wright. Born in Tallahassee in 1957. Graduated from the University of Miami, with dual degrees in journalism and political science, in 1979. Worked for a weekly newspaper in Apalache Springs."

"Who owned it?"

"Prescott Communications. That's how I managed to put this particular woman together with Judge Hoffman. His wife Eva—or ex-wife or whatever you want to call her—was the daughter of Prescott himself. I figured that couldn't be a coincidence."

"Go on," Kate said.

"Anyway, Adams worked at that paper for ten years or so. She must've been ambitious. She went from reporter to editor to publisher in a decade. In 1991, she moved over to Prescott Communication's corporate headquarters. Divorced her husband, Gary, that year."

"Why?"

"Loveless marriage? I don't know."

"Did you look at the filings?"

"I couldn't. Her county doesn't have those cases online.

You can verify names, dates, case numbers, and basic docket information, but it ends there. You'd have to go to the courthouse and dig the files up out of the archive if you want them. It doesn't say why they were divorced. I'll email what I have for you, though."

"That'd be great. What else do you have?"

"She kept moving up for a few more years. When the company chairman, William Prescott, ran for senator, she worked as a communications assistant on his campaign. I found her name on a couple of press releases. But Prescott lost the election and it looks like Adams left politics and newspapers behind."

He paused for a moment and Kate heard the clatter of his keyboard.

"The last entry I found on her, and this stretches back a ways, was her signing on to a firm called WP Properties. There was a small announcement on the business page of one of the local newspapers. If she's had any sort of career since then, she's kept it low profile, and it looks to me like she was on a downward slope. Which isn't surprising, considering what she went through."

Kate's brow furrowed. "What does that mean?"

"She took a couple of hits to her personal life. A year after she and her husband divorced, he died of an overdose. Alcohol and sleeping pills. And at some point, during Prescott's campaign, her daughter drowned."

"Jesus," Kate said.

"There were a few articles about it at the time. Supposedly, they were on a fishing trip off the coast of Florida. The little girl fell off the boat and drowned. Body was never recovered. Investigators eventually wrote it off as a tragic accident."

In spite of the heat, a cold sensation raced down Kate's

spine and she felt lightheaded.

"What was the little girl's name?" she asked.

"Jennifer. Jennifer Adams."

26

CLIMBING OUT OF THE RAMBLER, Kate headed for the room and checked her phone for Nava's email as she walked.

He had included Barbara Adams's current address along with an attached file.

Opening the attachment, she saw an old newspaper article and photo under the headline AREA GIRL DIES IN DROWNING.

She scanned the article and saw it was a recap of what Nava had told her. Jennifer Adams had been on a deep-sea fishing trip with her mother and some friends when she fell off the boat and drowned.

Her body never was found.

Using her thumb and index finger, Kate enlarged the picture to get a look at Jennifer, and though she had been expecting this, she felt another chill run through her.

It was the girl in Weston's drawing. The girl who had invited herself into Christopher's mind and put Kate down with a psychic one-two punch.

Wide grin, full cheeks, freckles. The only discernible difference was in the eyes. There was none of the terror. Instead, they were narrowed slightly with amusement, her nose wrinkled by her smile.

Weston was waiting for her outside his room, resting against the small ledge of his window, bottled water gripped in his hand, its bottom resting on his upper thigh. A second bottle, still unopened, sat next to him on the sill.

"Is Chris resting?" Kate asked.

"He's in the bathroom." Weston scooped up the bottle from the sill and handed it to her. "Was that your friend Nava on the phone?"

She nodded, opened the bottle and took a long pull, staring out at the parking lot. "We've got a real problem on our hands."

"Just one?"

She told him what Nava had found as she showed him the photo of Jennifer.

"Christ," he said. "So I was right. We *are* dealing with a spirit."

"And like Chris told us, she's angry." Kate paused. "I don't know why, but when I was talking to Angela Lowenthal this morning, I suddenly had this feeling that Jennifer was someone connected to John. It just came to me out of nowhere, like someone had implanted it in my brain. And when I mentioned her name, you should've seen Lowenthal's reaction."

"Maybe there's more to this girl's death than a simple drowning. Do we know where her mother is? She still alive?"

Kate nodded again. "Nava gave me her address."

"Maybe she can fill in some blanks," Weston said. "And if she can do that, we might be able to figure a way to stop what her daughter's been doing to Chris. Or at least figure out why." He paused. "While you were on the phone, I was sitting here thinking about Hoffman and the Harbinger and that letter he sent."

"And?"

"The guy's a nut job."

A faint smile formed on Kate's lips. "Nice diagnosis, doctor. But you're assuming it's just one guy. Don't forget what Chris said when John was found. That there two of them and one of them was a girl."

"Jennifer? After what she did to you…"

"No, he said Jennifer *told* him that, remember? She's the transmitter and he's the receiver."

"She also nearly put him in a coma, so I'll take what she has to say with a grain of salt." He paused. "Anyway, I was thinking about some of the things the Harbinger's letter said. The stuff about getting rid of the garbage. And what else? 'The streets will run red'?"

"He's already making that happen."

Weston nodded. "Same with the 'reckoning for the damned' part. He's definitely making people pay for their sins. But there was also a line about death to all creators who came before. That doesn't make any sense to me. What creators? Gods? Parents? Artists? I don't get it."

"Like you said… nut job. And maybe more than one."

"Right, but what's that part got to do with his usual choice of targets?"

Kate took a sip of water and shrugged. "Your guess is as good as mine."

"And how does Hoffman fit in? With those circumpuncts

at both scenes, that more or less proves the Harbinger killed him. But why? I'll give Miller credit for getting it right, but there has to be a better explanation than the killer wanting to punish the task force for going after the wrong guy. That's complete nonsense."

"Exactly what I've been thinking," Kate said. "And how did the Harbinger do it? I mean, John didn't take much of a swing at those cops who pulled him over, and we'll probably never know why. Maybe he was just too damn drunk to do anything else. But I doubt with his skills, as rusty as they may have been, he would've allowed himself to be taken by a serial killer."

"And yet it looks like he did," Weston said.

Kate thought about this. "You remember what else Christopher told us at the murder scene? That he didn't feel any fear coming from Hoffman?"

Weston nodded. "Just sadness. That he was hurting emotionally and physically."

"He also drove to that neighborhood because he wanted to. The neighbors saw him casing the block."

"So he may have been there to meet someone. Or was lured somehow."

Kate took another moment to think about it all, knowing that coincidences were rare and that everything that had happened before and since they arrived in Apalache Springs had to be linked somehow. And it all centered around John Hoffman.

Then suddenly it started to come together, the pieces of the puzzle dropping into place as she tried to recall a pair of names from the past.

"Kyle and Rebecca," she said.

Weston frowned. "Who?"

"Remember what Hoffman told me at the courthouse? He

was here because he needed to fix something. Something to do with his kids. Their names were Kyle and Rebecca."

"But I thought they disappeared," Weston said. "Along with their mother."

She nodded. "On a vacation here in Florida. And I don't think anything nefarious happened to them. I think they *wanted* to disappear."

"But why? And how?"

"The 'how' is the easy part. Eva's family has money and influence. But the 'why' is the biggest question mark. Miller asked me if John was a wife beater, but I didn't believe that for a second." She shook her head. "But maybe I misjudged him. He could have been that or something worse. And he had a lot of influence of his own. Could be that Eva was so afraid of him, or the people he might hire, that she did whatever she could to keep from being found. Her own family-financed witness protection program."

"Where are you going with this?"

"Kyle and Rebecca are grown now. Their mother can't control what they do. And maybe they weren't too happy with dear old dad. Maybe that line about death to creators has special significance to them. Grain of salt or not, Christopher—or Jennifer—may have had it right. What if John was lured to that house by his own goddamned kids?"

Weston raised his hands. "Wait a minute, slow down. You're saying you think his kids butchered him?"

"That's exactly what I'm saying."

"But... wouldn't that make *them* the Harbinger?"

Yes, it would. Christopher said.

He had appeared in the doorway of their room, his hair mussed and his arms folded tightly over his chest.

They both looked at him.

Jennifer heard you talking and wanted me to tell you

you're right. But you got the 'why' part wrong.

Kate took a step forward. "Is she here now, listening?"

Yes.

"What does she mean I got the 'why' part wrong? Can we talk to her?"

Christopher shook his head.

She won't. Not yet. She says you need to talk to her mother first.

"But why?"

She says Mommy knows what happened. That Mommy has always known what happened. So, Mommy should have to tell you.

27

THE APARTMENT BUILDING WAS YOUR standard-issue tenement on the city's east side. Peeling paint. Laundry hanging from balcony rails. The smell of urine and vomit and garbage rising from the alleyways on either side.

The second floor hallway reeked of kitchen grease, sweat, and more urine. Kate also thought she detected a hint of pot wafting on the air, and saw by Weston's expression that he was enjoying the ambience as much as she was.

Maybe she should've stayed in the car with Chris.

She knocked on the door of Barbara Adams's apartment.

From inside, she heard someone curse, followed by the feet of a chair scooting across a bare floor as someone rose to answer the door.

Kate glanced at Weston who stood at her side, smiling. His arms hung in front of him, his left hand loosely gripping his right wrist. He looked handsome, yet harmless and approachable.

Kate could imagine him going door to door, handing out pamphlets for his church or meeting with clients as a businessman. Was she glimpsing the old Noah Weston? The one who hadn't been robbed of his family and livelihood? A man who believed that, if he lived right, good things would come his way, an unseen deity would protect him?

A man who didn't get out of bed each day fueled by his desire to hunt down and kill a madman?

Kate knew that version of Weston was gone, slain by the Beast just as surely as he'd killed Weston's wife and children. But apparently Weston had enough practice to fake it when necessary.

He noticed her staring at him.

"What?" he asked.

Before she could answer, the sound of an unlocking deadbolt distracted them both. The door opened and a wrinkled face appeared in the space between the jamb and the door. Kate noted two safety chains in place.

"Yes?" the woman asked.

Kate spoke first. "Are you Barbara Adams?"

The woman's eyes shifted from Kate to Weston and back to Kate. "Who are you?"

Even at a distance, Kate caught a whiff of alcohol on her breath.

"I'm Kate Messenger," she said. "And this is Noah Weston."

"What do you want?" Though age had robbed the woman's voice of its volume, Kate easily heard the barely restrained hostility in her tone.

"We'd like to speak with you," Kate said.

"I figured that much or you wouldn't be knocking on my

door, would you? Everybody wants something, so what do you want?"

"We need to ask you some questions."

"Why? Who are you?"

"I told you," Kate said.

"You told me your names, which doesn't mean a damn thing."

Weston released the grip on his wrist, reached into his shirt pocket, and withdrew a piece of paper folded into a rectangle.

"It's about your daughter," he said as he started to unfold it, and Kate realized it was the drawing of Jennifer.

"I have no idea what you're talking about."

"I think you do, Barbara."

"I really... I'm closing the door now."

Before she could, Weston reached forward and slid the unfolded paper through the gap. Adams snatched it from him and slammed the door closed, but seconds later they heard her inhale sharply and it swung open again.

She slipped her arm through the space between the door and the jamb. She'd crumpled the drawing in her fist and held it up a few inches from Weston's face.

"Did the Prescotts put you up to this?"

"No, ma'am," he said.

"You tell them this is a new low." She threw the paper at him. It struck his chest, bounced off and plummeted to the ground. "God damn them and God damn you for bringing it. I never said a word. Never."

Weston raised his hands in a gesture of surrender. "Ms. Adams, if you'd just calm down..."

"I kept my mouth shut for—what?—twenty years? Never said a word. Now you bring me this?" Tears streamed down her lined cheeks. She jabbed a finger at the discarded paper.

"You broke me. You took my baby. You threatened me! Go to hell! The Prescotts—"

Weston raised his voice. "Ma'am, we're not with the Prescotts."

"What?"

"I'm telling you, we're not with the Prescotts."

The door slammed closed again. From the other side, Kate could hear Adams undoing the security chains. This time she opened the door a little wider, but still didn't invite them in.

"You *must* be. No one else knows."

"We're not," Kate said. "I promise you that. Have they been in touch with you?"

"Yes."

"Often?"

Adams hesitated.

"How often are they contacting you?" Weston asked.

"Who are you again?"

Kate repeated their names. "We're looking into a couple of murders. And during the investigation your daughter's name came up."

Adams studied her uncertainly for a moment, then her fingers released the door and it swung inward. Her body sagged under an unseen weight, forcing her against the jamb.

"Oh, God," she said.

28

"ARE YOU THE POLICE?" Adams asked.

Before Kate could answer, Weston said, "We're investigators."

The woman nodded, apparently satisfied or afraid to ask for more information. "I knew this was going to happen someday."

Weston made a show of looking around the hallway before turning his eyes back to Adams.

"Are you comfortable talking about this out here?" he asked. "Maybe this isn't the best place for it."

There was no challenge in his tone. Just a nice guy looking out for her.

Adams stepped out of the doorway and waved them inside.

"Please," she said.

The apartment reeked of cat urine and booze. The curtains were pulled closed, shielding the interior from sunlight. A thick haze of cigarette smoke and dust hung in the air, making the place seem even darker, more suffocating.

Adams led them to a living room, then dropped into an armchair covered in a threadbare floral print fabric. She gathered up her cigarettes, tapped one into her hand, slid it into her mouth. She set the pack down, picked up a pink disposable lighter, thumbed it to life, and held the blue-yellow flame to the tip of the cigarette, torching it.

Kate noted the stacked newspapers lining either side of the hallway that led from the front door into the living room. The only other furniture was a small couch covered in the same fabric as the chair, a coffee table littered with dusty books and magazines, a couple of smaller tables, and a cheap tube television on a metal stand.

A single framed photo of Jennifer stood on the table next to Adams's chair.

Adams made a chopping motion in the direction of the couch.

"Please, sit," she said. Her voice sounded hollow and distracted.

They both declined. If it bothered her, she gave no outward hint. She hunched down in her seat, puffed on her cigarette, and fixed her eyes on a point on the wall behind Weston.

"On that drawing," she said. "You wrote, 'Sparkle.'"

Weston nodded.

"That's what I used to call her. Always. She loved it when I called her that." She swallowed hard and looked up at them, her eyes moist. "How did you know?"

Weston opened his mouth to speak, but Kate cut him off. She doubted he was going to dish about vengeful spirits, telepathy, and serial murderers, but she couldn't be sure.

"Barbara, I know this is difficult for you. I do. But we have to ask some questions. We don't have much time and we really need you to be as honest as possible. Okay?"

Adams nodded and puffed at her cigarette.

Kate said, "You told the police your daughter drowned. Is that true?"

"Yes, that's what I told them."

"But is it true?"

She pivoted her wrist, so the cigarette was vertical, and stared at its burning tip for a couple of heartbeats. She looked so exhausted by this sad sorry existence, that she could barely find the will to keep talking. Then something in her eyes shifted—a decision made—and she said, "They told me they'd kill me if I didn't keep quiet."

"Who told you that?"

"Prescott."

"He said he'd kill you?"

"He said he'd have me killed."

"And you believed him," Kate said.

"They murdered my child. She was a baby and they murdered her. Why wouldn't they kill me?"

Kate and Weston exchanged a look.

"Prescott's dead," she said. "You know that, right?"

"Of course."

"But you're still scared."

"Wouldn't you be? His money's still out there. He has foundations, loyalists, heirs, libraries named after him. He has a network of people. I'll never be safe."

"Barbara, help me out. If Prescott's dead, he obviously hasn't been threatening you. So who is? This is important."

Adams closed her eyes and stroked her cheek in small circles. Heaving a sigh, she flicked some cigarette ash onto the floor. "He has a man, Jack Baker. Do you know Jack?"

"I've run into him once or twice."

"He's a bastard, an atrocious bastard." She dragged on the cigarette, exhaled a long stream of white-gray smoke. "He and that wench, Lowenthal, are in contact with me all the time. They always want to know if I've been... If I've been a good girl. If I've talked to anyone about my little Sparkle."

She paused and seemed to go away for a moment, lost in a memory, then looked at Kate, confusion in her eyes.

"Who did you say you work for again?"

Kate could feel impatience welling up, but Weston seemed to sense this and said, "So, Prescott wanted your daughter's death to go away."

Stubbing out her cigarette, Adams shifted her gaze to him, looking as if she'd forgotten he was there.

She nodded. "He said he was doing it to protect his grandchildren, but he was doing it for himself. Some senator was supposed to retire and he wanted to run for office. The last thing he needed was a scandal. And if people found out about those... those fucking little..."

"You mean Kyle and Rebecca Hoffman?" Kate asked.

"Hell, yes, that's who I mean." She reached over and grabbed her cigarettes. "I've never seen anything like those two. And, God willing, I never will. They came out the previous summer and they were great kids. The next year..." Her voice trailed off.

"What about them?"

"They had changed. Oh, you wouldn't know it at first. They showed up with their expensive clothes and their smiles and their manners. But those kids were not right. Sparkle tried to tell me, but I wouldn't listen to her."

"What did she say?" Weston asked.

"That they were being mean to her, acting differently

around her than they did the adults. I didn't think she was lying. But kids can be sensitive. Jealous. They had things she didn't have."

"Did she say what they were doing?" Kate asked.

"No. Just that they were mean." She locked eyes with Kate. "God as my witness, I didn't know how they really were or I would've packed her up and left right then and there. I swear."

Kate nodded. She wasn't sure she believed Adams, but she wanted to keep her talking.

"I needed the job so I told her she was making things up. I told her she had to stop saying such things."

"And she did," Weston said.

By now tears were rolling down the woman's deeply lined face. Having jabbed another cigarette between her lips, she tossed aside the pack, lit the cigarette, and cast her eyes down at the floor.

She shook her head. "Jennifer wasn't the kind to suffer that sort of thing in silence. From what the Hoffman children said later, they'd been teasing her and she threatened to tell on them. So one of the kids—that damn boy, Kyle—grabbed a pipe he'd found in the garage. And he hit her. Again and again. His sister Rebecca sees this and she goes crazy. The little bitch started hitting Jennifer, too, with her fist. When they were done..."

Adams covered her face and she sobbed.

As Kate watched the woman cry, she felt a squeezing sensation around her own heart and a dull ache in her throat. She swallowed hard to clear it and said, "Why didn't you report the murder?"

Adams drew her hands from her face and looked at Kate as though she'd lost her mind. "Report it? To who? This is the Prescotts."

"The Prescotts aren't above the law," Kate said.

"You keep telling yourself that. I saw what happened to Judge Hoffman."

"He *knew* about this?"

Adams shook her head. "No. At least not twenty years ago. His wife, Eva, and old man Prescott hid the whole thing from him."

"Why the hell would they do that?" Noah asked.

The woman snorted. "You have to ask?"

She was leaning forward, forearms resting on her thighs. Grayish white smoke curled up from the cigarette, the end of which had burned nearly to the filter. She fixed them with a bloodshot stare.

"The judge probably was the only decent human being in that whole damn group. If he'd known what his children had done, what that bitch wife and her father wanted done, he never would've stood for it. Never."

Kate said, "That's why she took the kids and disappeared."

Adams nodded. "She knew the judge would call the police, the FBI, whatever it took, to get justice for my daughter. He wouldn't look the other way, even if it meant putting his own kids on trial. So her father bought some property outside Tallahassee and set them up there. Really, he paid the money and his lawyers set the whole thing up."

"Richelson, Taylor and Ward?" Kate asked.

The woman nodded. "Yes, them. They folded that one property in with a couple dozen others. Made it harder to find."

Kate held up her hands.

"Wait a minute," she said, "John loved those kids. How did he not know they were crazy enough to kill someone? That makes no sense."

"That's not an easy one to answer," Adams told her.

She dragged once more on her cigarette and blew twin lines of smoke from her nostrils as she ground it out in the ashtray. With a grunt, she pushed herself up from the chair, collected her coffee cup, and shuffled into the kitchen. She tossed the cup's contents into the sink and refilled it with fresh brew from the carafe.

Standing on her tiptoes, she reached into a cabinet located above her sink, rummaged around for a couple of heartbeats.

Kate felt her body start to tense. "What are you looking for, Barbara?"

Adams brought down a bottle of Irish cream whiskey and showed it to them. "You want some?"

Kate relaxed. She and Weston shook their heads.

Shrugging, Adams unscrewed the top, splashed liquor into the cup, resealed the bottle, and stowed it in the cabinet.

"How did Hoffman not know Kyle and Rebecca were dangerous?" Kate asked again. "Kids don't just suddenly turn into vicious killers. There are signs."

Adams raised the cup to her lips, and blew on its steaming contents.

"Lady, I don't have an answer for that. Those kids came to Florida every year and they'd always been polite to a fault. I swear their father had put the fear of God into them somehow. I'd never seen two better behaved children. I know it's probably hard for you to believe, knowing what you do, but I wouldn't have let those kids around my daughter if I'd thought they were dangerous. I'm not a monster."

"No one said you were."

"But they'd always been very sweet and kind. I'd never had any issues with them. Then they showed up that year and it was like they were two different kids. They'd act normal, then I'd see them when they didn't know I was looking, and they had this... gleam in their eyes, not crazy, just—I don't know—like a couple of predators. I didn't know what to think."

Adams fell silent, turned to the freezer, opened it, and rooted around for ice. Her hand came out clutching a couple of cubes, both of which she dropped in her drink. Kate heard the ice cubes snap when they hit the hot coffee. She wheeled back around and took a sip.

"I kept telling myself I was overreacting. Or imagining things." She slurped more coffee. "There was no way they could've changed that much and so quickly, I told myself."

She squeezed her eyes shut, but kept talking.

"I guess I should've listened to my intuition. But I had no reason to think there was anything wrong."

"When did you see them change?" Weston asked.

The woman was raising her cup to her lips. She paused and looked over the rim at him. "This had to be twenty years ago."

Alarms rang in Kate's head. She glanced at Weston, saw his taut expression and figured he was thinking the same thing.

"That's not what I meant," he said to Adams. "*When* twenty years ago did you notice the change? Was it right after they arrived? Later?"

She closed her eyes and pressed her lips tightly together. Her head bobbed slightly, as though she was trying to jar the memories loose.

"After they got here," she said. "Definitely after they got here. They were supposed to stay for—hell, I don't remember—six weeks? Two months? Something like that. They weren't at the house much, though. They visited a couple of their grandfather's newspapers. He chartered a boat and took them fishing. Took two of his photographers along to get pictures."

"Two photographers?" Kate said.

"He'd already hired a political consultant—some oily guy out of Jacksonville; I can't remember his name—who'd told him to get lots of pictures with his family, in case they needed them for the campaign."

"Who were the photographers?"

"Jerry Sherman and David Warwick. They both worked for the Tallahassee newspaper. They'd been there for years, if I remember right. It's been a long time."

Kate made a mental note. The names meant nothing to her, but she figured she could ask Cindy Davis about the photographers later.

Kate noticed Adams's eyes were bloodshot, the lids drooping. She guessed the drinks were starting to take their toll and soon the woman would pass out.

"Yes, the photographers followed Prescott everywhere. His grandchildren, too. After awhile, it got to where we didn't even notice them. They were just more hired hands as far as the house staff was concerned. We tried to stay out of their way as best we could, but sometimes we ended up in the pictures. I wasn't too sure about that, but Mr. Prescott's consultant loved that sort of thing.

"Everyone was a good sport about it. Except for one young man. He'd been a security guard at one of the newspaper offices. When Mr. Prescott's driver fell ill, his people sent this man over."

Kate's pulse accelerated. "Do you remember his name? Please tell me you remember his name."

Adams blinked at her. "Who's name?"

"The security guard. The one who didn't want to be photographed."

"You're kidding me, right? That was twenty years ago. He

was a big man, I do remember that. But his name...?" She shook her head, then paused suddenly. "Wait a minute. Maybe I do remember, but only because he always scared me a little. I think his name was... Mitchell, or... no, no, no. Mickey. His name was Mickey."

"Bonner?" Kate asked.

The woman paused and thought about it a couple of seconds before nodding.

"Yes," she said. "That's it. Mickey Bonner."

29

KATE SAID, "YOU KNOW WHAT THIS means, don't you?"

"Yeah, that there may be pictures of the Beast out there."

They had left Adams's apartment several minutes earlier and were standing in the lobby of her building, next to some mailboxes built into the wall.

Kate had tried asking Adams more questions, but with each answer, the woman's voice had slurred more, her thoughts growing more unfocused. By the time they'd excused themselves, she had settled back into her chair and was staring at the blank television, barely acknowledging them.

"We need to get those pictures," Weston said. "Should we call the newspaper?"

"I have another idea."

Retrieving her phone from her purse, Kate called Cindy

Davis to ask if she knew anything about the photographers, and if their photos from that period could have been archived. If there was a photo of Bonner among them and they age-progressed it, they'd have a better idea of how he looked today.

But Davis didn't answer, so Kate left a message on her voicemail.

She looked at Weston, who was staring at the ceiling, as though he could see into Adams's apartment.

"Maybe we should call Detective Miller," she said.

"And tell him what? A drunk woman who decades ago claimed her daughter drowned now says the girl was the victim of murder and a cover up? Why am I thinking he won't buy that?"

"Do you buy it?" Kate asked.

"A hundred percent. You saw what happened to that poor bastard in Alabama by the time the Beast got done with him. If Hoffman's kids had contact with Bonner, there's no reason to think it wouldn't have changed them. And he may've had a lot of fun doing it."

"Yeah," Kate said. "And I keep thinking about Rusty Patterson. He had contact with Bonner, too. Right after my mother was murdered."

"The guy's a goddamned virus. And he needs to be eradicated."

"Well, we won't be able to accomplish that today. But maybe we can clean up one of his messes."

Raising her phone, she dialed Angela Lowenthal's number.

•

Kate left Lowenthal three voicemails in as many hours, none of which the attorney returned. She'd kept them vague, not wanting to tip her hand.

On the fourth one, she decided to go for broke.

Seated on the edge of her bed, she listened to Lowenthal's now-familiar voicemail greeting and tapped her foot impatiently.

Weston was leaning against a wall, arms crossed over his chest, watching her. Christopher sat nearby, eating takeout chili Weston had bought for dinner.

Once Lowenthal stopped speaking and the tone sounded, Kate said, "This is Kate Messenger. I know about Jennifer Adams and Hoffman's kids." She paused. "I also know you, Jack Baker, and your firm have been covering this up. Call me now or I'm calling the FBI."

She clicked off and set the phone on her nightstand. She glanced at Weston, then watched Chris slurp at the chili, which couldn't have been easy with less than half a tongue.

Kate's phone pinged. She snatched it up from the nightstand and saw she'd received a text message. She tried to ignore the cold fist thudding into her gut as she read it.

She set the phone aside and looked up at Weston. "That was Lowenthal. She says she wants to meet us."

"She give you a time and place?"

"Yes, but I don't recognize the address. It's not her office."

"Probably some nice out-of-the-way spot where they can deal with us."

"Maybe I should call Miller. Or even Page and Jefferson."

NO!

The voice cut through Kate's mind, the pain forcing her to slap her hands to the sides of her head and groan. "Jesus, Christopher."

She looked over at him. His face was turned toward her, but his expression flat.

No police. No FBI.

"It's a deathtrap," she said.

Deal with it, bitch.

Kate's heart went cold. "Jennifer?"

You three go. No police. No FBI.

"Why would we do that?" Weston asked.

Christopher blinked and shook his head.

She won't talk to you anymore. Not unless you do what she says. And if you keep asking questions, she said she'll hurt me.

Kate's hands balled into fists and she cursed under her breath. Taking orders—quite possibly fatal ones—from an angry spirit seemed like the height of lunacy.

Yet, how could they refuse?

"All right" she said. "We'll go."

30

WESTON BRAKED THE RAMBLER, EASED it onto a gravel shoulder, then killed the engine and headlights. Night had fallen and the full moon provided the only light.

Off to their left stood the grounds of a sprawling estate that Lowenthal's text had directed them to, and it looked as if it had seen better days. The grounds were covered by densely packed cypress trees, their roots exposed, the tree-tops interlocking with one another.

Kate guessed the canopy of leaves blocked most of the moonlight from ever reaching the house and its grounds. Which may or may not have been a good thing.

She and Weston had no intention of driving up to the front gate and ringing the bell, in hopes that Angela Lowenthal or Jack Baker would greet them with a smile. The darkness would make it easier to approach the old house. But it would also make it easy for someone to attack them before they ever saw it coming.

Slipping off her seatbelt, Kate turned and regarded Christopher, who sat in his usual spot on the backseat. He was quiet and still, and she knew that Jennifer's angry spirit still exerted control over his mind and body, and could hurt him—and even those around him—whenever she damn well pleased.

Kate had no idea how to stop the girl and that scared the hell out of her. But she hoped that coming here would help satisfy Jennifer's need, whatever it might be, and put an end to this.

"I don't like the idea of leaving you here alone," Kate said.

The boy acknowledged her with a curt nod.

"If you need anything," Weston told him, "you contact us. You got that, son?"

He nodded again.

If she'll let me.

Those four words made Kate's stomach flutter, and she noted that Weston looked a little pale. He never spoke about such things, but she knew that Christopher was very much a son to him now, and the concern in his eyes was palpable. He had to be thinking of his daughters, and the loss he felt when they were taken from him.

If he were to lose Christopher as well, she couldn't predict how he might react.

But Jennifer had demanded they come here, and here they all were, hoping the night would bring her story to a close.

She looked again at the house and the dark grounds.

Back at the motel, Kate had remembered Barbara Adams saying that the Prescotts had sent Kyle and Rebecca Hoffman to live in a home outside Tallahassee, and she had wondered if this was the place. She had then called Adams from the room phone and run the address past her.

Adams, who still sounded drunk, confirmed that, yes, this was the very same place. So, just before dusk, Kate had made sure they weren't being tailed by the FBI and they cruised past the property to give them a better idea of what they were walking into.

What they'd found had told them little. An asphalt driveway pocked with holes, flanked on either side by concrete walls, long sections of which were curtained with kudzu. The uncovered parts looked weathered and cracked, but still sturdy enough. A wrought-iron gate shielded the entrance, and an old guard shack, a rectangular box no larger than a phone booth, stood next to it. The rest of the perimeter was covered by a tall chain-link fence topped with razor wire.

In the light, it had looked to Kate like equal parts asylum and prison.

That was no accident.

From what they'd learned about Hoffman's children, they needed to be kept away from society—or at least watched closely. This estate would have accomplished that, of course. But Kate figured the security was also a way to keep Hoffman out, should he ever figure out where to look. Kate still wasn't sure whether he'd gotten that far in his search or whether he'd nailed it down to just a general geographic area. She might never know. And right now, she wasn't sure whether that mattered.

She turned to Weston. "Let's go."

She popped open the Rambler's door. Its metal hinge screeched, setting Kate's teeth on edge. The rhythmic clicking of insects permeated the air, and Kate guessed the squeak seemed louder than it was. But she also knew that for someone who had spent time here and knew its native sounds, the squeaking of a hinge could stand out like a bomb blast.

Keeping her Beretta gripped tightly at her side, she and Weston stalked toward the chain-link security fence, Weston carrying a duffel he'd taken from the back of the Rambler. He drifted within a couple of feet of her and she waved him away, reminding him they didn't want to be clustered together if someone started shooting.

Nodding his understanding, he moved left to grab some distance, but Kate felt doubt gnawing at her. Weston had courage and a keen intellect and had dedicated his life to tracking the Beast. While she had made it clear to him that she preferred to try to take the Beast alive when they finally managed to catch up with him, she was also realistic about such things, which meant Weston might be forced to spill blood. And his refusal to carry a gun complicated matters.

If her instincts were right, tonight was no different, and if Lowenthal had Baker and his men lying in wait, things could get very ugly.

She didn't question Weston's resolve or his intensity of purpose.

But if it came down to it, could he kill?

If he hesitated, the results could be catastrophic—for all of them.

Kate pushed these thoughts aside and told herself to focus. Weston pulled the duffel bag from his shoulder, laid it on the ground next to the chain-link fence and knelt beside it. Unzipping the bag, he slipped a hand inside and pulled out a pair of gloves and some wire cutters. He slid the gloves on and began snipping at the fence.

Kate stood over him. She swept her eyes over their surroundings, but she couldn't find much more than shadows. While she wished she could use the Mini-Mag in her pocket, she and Weston had already decided not to use their flashlights except in an emergency.

She glanced at Weston and saw he'd cut part of a semi-circle through the fence. Even in the dull light, she could see sweat glisten on the skin of his forearms. She felt perspiration gather on the back of her neck, then trickle under her shirt collar, down the curve of her spine, and was well aware that Jack Baker and his goons could appear at any moment.

Weston finished cutting the fence. Weaving his gloved fingers into it, he peeled aside the cut section, exposing a hole roughly three feet wide and two feet high. Returning the wire cutters to the bag, he zipped it shut, pushed it through the hole and followed it through.

She crawled through after him, and once they were back on their feet, they moved through the cypress trees, Kate again gesturing for Weston to keep his distance from her. They walked for several minutes before the canopy of trees seemed to evaporate and they found themselves in the main compound of the estate, which was bathed in moonlight.

Ahead, they saw a circular driveway with an old fountain at its center. Weeds and tall grass covered any parts of the property not covered by concrete or asphalt.

The house stood to their left, a hundred yards or so away from them. Graffiti marred the exterior walls. Plywood panels covered most of the first floor windows. A few windows gaped open, the glass panes long shattered.

Weston signaled to her and pointed at the second floor. Kate looked up and saw a dim glow emanating from one of the windows. Kate also heard a mechanical hum coming from inside the house. She guessed it was a generator.

She and Weston melted back into the tree line, using it to cover their approach as they followed the driveway around toward the house.

Kate was surprised by the disrepair. If the Prescott family

had wanted to keep the property, why hadn't they maintained it? They had the money.

It was as though Eva and her children had simply fled, leaving it to rot and ruin.

Had they run from something? Someone? Had they needed to disappear again? If so, why keep the property?

It made no damned sense to Kate.

As they closed in on the house, a horrible smell filled the air. Kate wrinkled her nose involuntarily and quickly realized why. Piled in the driveway were dozens, maybe a couple hundred, bags of garbage.

Someone had been living here for awhile.

Sticking to the trees, they circled around to the rear of the mansion. A pool lay just behind. A small outbuilding that probably had once housed the pumps and motors for the pool was covered in graffiti. The door had been torn open and hung from a single hinge. Kate smelled stagnant water and rotting vegetation.

They broke from the trees and moved toward the house. Kate glanced at Weston and saw him reach into the duffel and pull out a crowbar.

Not much, but at least it was something.

As this thought vacated Kate's mind, a scream rang out in the darkness. Her heart skipped and blood thundered in her ears.

Weston shot her a look.

Nodding, she sprinted with him toward the house.

31

WHEN THEY REACHED THE BACK door, Kate tried the handle, but found it locked.

"Step back," Weston said.

Kate stepped to the side, wondering what he had in mind. Before she could ask the question, he heaved the duffel bag filled with tools through the window just above the knob.

The pane of glass burst with a loud pop. The bag disappeared into darkness and Kate heard the tinkling of glass shards striking the floor intermingled with the clatter of metal tools hitting tile.

Weston reached an arm through the window, snapped open the latch, and swung the open door inward.

Jesus, Kate thought. When this was over, the two of them would have to have a long talk about the concept of stealth.

If they survived.

Once inside, they found themselves in a large room, lit by wan moonlight that filtered in through a broken window. Its walls were lined with shelves that carried ancient can goods, the labels peeling away.

Weston took a step forward, but Kate pushed past him, her arm raised, Beretta leading the way.

The pantry led into a room Kate pegged as the kitchen. Appliances had been stripped away and cabinet doors torn off. The wood flooring was curved in spots or had peeled away and the room stank of mildew.

Kate guessed vandals had stripped out the copper plumbing before the water had been turned off, leaving the place flooded. After the economy went belly up several years ago, she had seen the same thing in vacant houses in Santa Flora. People stripped out the copper plumbing to sell it for scrap yards.

Kate strained her ears, hoping to catch some sign of any occupants. The place had gone quiet. No more screams.

She assumed this was because of Weston's boneheaded play, breaking out that window. Whoever was here now knew they weren't alone.

They cleared the kitchen and found themselves in a large room with a vaulted ceiling and a skylight. The moon's glow filtered through the glass, much brighter here, lighting the room, which reeked of mildew, urine, and feces.

Kate caught traces of another smell, one she'd become all too familiar with as a cop: the stench of death. The smell permeated the air as though it'd been absorbed into the wall panels and floors.

Kate felt the contents of her stomach pushing up and the room swayed. She sucked in a deep pull of the rotten air through her mouth, steadied herself.

She heard Weston gag and shot him a *don't you dare* look.

He jabbed an elbow into her upper arm, flicked his flashlight on and pointed the beam, gesturing for her to look.

She saw a face staring back at her and gasped.

In life, Jack Baker's eyes had conveyed a cruelty and arrogant detachment Kate had seen in dozens of offenders. She'd noted it when he'd kicked her out of that office building, and had even caught a hint of it earlier, when she'd encountered him at the arraignment with Hoffman and Lowenthal.

Death had left those eyes dull and unfocused as they stared back at her, the tanned skin of his forehead split open, rivulets of fresh blood oozing across his forehead, his yellow-white hair flecked with crimson.

Kate just stood there, stunned. Baker had been the threat they had expected to encounter here, so what the hell did this mean?

Part of her—arguably the sane part—wanted to flee this place. To run until she made it back to the Rambler.

But she knew better. Until they knew why Jennifer had demanded they come here, Christopher was in danger.

And from the look of things, he wasn't the only one.

They reached the stairs. Kate took the lead, ascending them slowly. By some miracle, she'd grown accustomed to the horrible stench pervading this section of the house. She guessed she had adrenaline to thank for that.

As they reached the halfway point, her gaze was parallel with the second floor. Artificial light leaked from somewhere down the hall, sending a dull, yellow glow fanning across the threadbare carpet.

A generator hummed from somewhere on this floor. Kate guessed they'd placed it in another room with an open window so the fumes could escape. Over its mechanical hum, she heard voices murmuring.

By the time they reached the second floor landing, the voices had grown louder. Not yet discernible, but she could tell that one was male, the other female.

And that could only mean one thing.

As she stepped forward, she was faintly aware of her hand tightening on the sweat-slicked grip of her Beretta. Weston was at her side now, and she glanced down and saw the crowbar still clutched in his hand.

They crept through the hallway, staying close to the wall, several open doors on either side. She glanced inside the rooms as they passed them, saw they had been stripped of furniture.

At the far end of the hall, facing them directly, was a single, half-closed door, yellow light spilling into the hallway.

Just before Kate reached it, she heard a pained yelp followed by someone thudding to the floor.

Muttering a curse, she picked up the pace and carefully peered through the space between the door jamb and the door.

Angela Lowenthal lay on the floor inside, a crimson stain blossoming on the shoulder of her white blouse. Her hair was matted against the side of her head where a dark spot was forming.

A slender man knelt next to her, clutching a length of galvanized pipe that was slick with blood.

His head was completely shaved, but he wasn't wearing his sunglasses.

It was the man she'd seen at the courthouse. The man who had stolen the judge's satchel. And without the sunglasses, she immediately saw the resemblance in his feral blue eyes.

John's son. Kyle Hoffman.

Staring down at Lowenthal, he suddenly brought the pipe

up, his lips twisting into a lustful grin.

Shit.

Kate drew back her foot and fired it forward, slamming it against the door. It swung inward, and she stepped inside, hearing Weston's footsteps follow her into the room big enough to house an entire family as she leveled the Beretta's muzzle at Kyle.

"Put it down!" she shouted. "Step away from her!"

Kyle shot her a look and hesitated, the pipe raised just above his head.

Kate's breath hung in her throat and her heart pounded.

Was this guy a dead ender or a killer who wanted to survive? Maybe one smart enough to know his family's wealth would afford him good, expensive lawyers.

Lawyers like Lowenthal, whose breathing sounded shallow.

"Don't shoot," Kyle said calmly.

His hand lowered slowly and he set the pipe on the ground.

Then he smiled as his gaze drifted past Kate.

From behind, she heard the sounds of a scuffle.

Fuck.

She threw back a glance and saw Weston struggling with a wild woman. She held onto him like a rabid wolverine, the fingers of one hand tangled in his hair, the other wrestling him for the crowbar.

Rebecca Hoffman was smaller than Weston, but her ferocity was making up for that.

Kate looked at Kyle, to make sure he was a good distance away, then shot forward toward Weston. But before she could reach him, pain suddenly bolted through her skull.

She staggered, her legs carrying her a couple more steps before they turned to rubber and she crashed to the ground, landing on her knees.

A surge of pain, this one even more intense, seared her mind and turned her vision fuzzy.

Squeezing her eyes closed, she clenched her jaw to keep from screaming. The agony, though intense, was familiar.

It was the same pain she'd felt outside Hoffman's crime scene.

It sizzled through her spine, her pelvis, legs and feet. It felt as though someone was pouring molten steel into her, the hot liquid scorching her insides, vaporizing the contents of her body.

Every inch of her felt as though it was ablaze, her muscles, her nerves no longer responding to her.

Her vision turned dark.

Was this how it felt to die? To be dead? An eternity spent with her flesh afire and panicked thoughts careening through her head?

As she writhed on the floor, her mind began to slow and a single thought came together.

A thought that wasn't hers.

I'm baaaaack…

Jennifer. It was Jennifer.

Kate's eyes cleared in time to see Kyle surging toward her, the pipe back in his hand. She heard the guttural noise escaping his throat as he bore down on her. She had dropped her Beretta and her hands rose up, empty—

—except *she* wasn't the one who had made them do that.

She had no control of her body at all.

Jennifer did.

I'm baaaaack.

I'm baaaaaaaaaaaack.

I'm back. I'm back. I'm back.

Kyle was almost upon her.

Kate's head involuntarily snapped left then right, where she spotted her Beretta laying on the floor. She lunged for it, slapping her hand down on top of the weapon, fingers curling around the grip.

As her hands swung it around toward Kyle, he suddenly stopped, frozen in place, his gaze on the weapon.

She heard another voice. *Her* voice this time, the words delivered in a sing-song fashion, pitch running low to high. The melody simple, a child's song.

"I'm baaaack, Kyle."

He frowned. "And who the fuck are you?"

"You remember me, don't you?"

"All I know is you look like a—"

Her finger squeezed the trigger and a sharp crack filled the room. The slug hurtled from the pistol's muzzle and pierced the fabric of Kyle's pant leg, drilling into the soft flesh of his thigh.

Blood sprang up from the wound and Kyle staggered, fingers uncurling, the pipe falling to the floor. He stumbled toward her, his face twisted with pain. He tried to stand, but his injured leg couldn't support the weight and he crumpled to the carpet.

Kate got to her feet and walked toward him, her steps slow, steady. There was no hesitation there, just a desire to enjoy every second of his suffering.

"Doesn't feel so good, does it?" she said.

Kyle held his hand against his thigh, blood seeping between his fingers. "Who *are* you?"

"How could you not remember me, Kyle? I was your graduation gift to Rebecca. When you two went from killing cats and jack rabbits to murdering little girls."

It took Kyle a moment for the realization to cross his face.

Then he understood. He knew exactly who Kate was.

"*What?*" he cried. "How is this even possible?"

"Don't worry about possible. Just worry about dying."

Her leg shot out and she drove her heel into his wounded thigh, eliciting an anguished scream. He tried to retaliate by kicking at her with his good leg, but she sidestepped it and his eyes went wide.

Kate wanted to order him to stay on the ground. She wanted to tie his hands, search him for more weapons, and call for the police.

But she couldn't. She had no choice in the matter.

She heard the voice again.

Her voice.

Not her words.

"Bye bye, Kyle. Maybe we'll see each other in Hell."

Her finger squeezed the trigger three more times. The gunshots blended into a single peal of thunder, the muzzle flashes illuminating Kyle's face, which was contorted into a mask of terror. Slugs drilled into his chest, dotting his shirt with crimson blossoms.

The guy was dead, and a warm sense of satisfaction washed over Kate. It wasn't *her* emotion, but she could feel it nonetheless.

She heard a scream behind her. She wheeled around, the gun raised, and spotted Rebecca and Weston now staring at her, no longer struggling. There were scratches on Weston's face, the crowbar still in his hand as he stood back and away from Rebecca.

Who was now holding a knife.

Where it had come from was anyone's guess.

She clenched it tightly, the blade shifting between Kate and Weston, her eyes wide at the sight of her brother's lifeless body, terror etching her face.

Kate pointed the Beretta at Rebecca, and another a warm

sensation washed through her body.

Staring at her in disbelief, Weston held up his free hand, gesturing for her to stop. "Kate... What the hell are you doing? You just *executed* that guy."

"Oh, don't be such a cry baby," she heard herself say. "Kyle was a really bad boy and he deserved what he got." She looked at Rebecca. "And so does *she*."

"What the hell is going on with you?"

"I'm just taking care of business." She felt herself smile and her finger tightened on the trigger. "The bitch knows what I mean. Don't you, Rebecca?"

Rebecca was shaking her head, the tears streaming down her face barely masking her fury. "You... You just killed my brother, you bitch. My Kyle..."

"Oh, boo-hoo, Beckykins. Where were the tears when you watched him bash my head in? How many people have you killed since then, huh? How many mothers has your family threatened, like they did mine?"

Kate saw that same sudden realization cross Rebecca's face. The knowing, mixed with bewilderment. How could this be possible?

Weston tensed and raised his hands slightly, and Kate saw that he also knew exactly what was going on.

"Jesus Christ," he murmured. "Jennifer?"

"Who else would I be, silly?"

Rebecca uttered one word. "But—"

Then the gun barked and a slug tore into her torso, spinning her ninety degrees, before she collapsed in a boneless heap, the knife clattering on the floor next to her.

Weston stared in stunned disbelief.

Kate laughed, a high-pitched thing that didn't quite sound natural, and his expression morphed from shock to anger. He started to speak, but Kate gestured with the gun for him to stay quiet.

"Don't do anything to make me mad, Noah." She nodded to Rebecca, then Kyle. "Look what happens to people who make me mad. They did bad things to me. They did bad things to a lot of girls, and I made them pay."

Giggling, she drifted to one side, circling around toward Weston and prompting him to fall into orbit with her. She waggled the gun at him.

"I know all about you, you know. I know what happened to *your* little girls."

Weston tensed again. "And how do you know that?"

"Shame, shame," she said. "You were out being bad, Noah. You were doing dirty things with a dirty lady and you made the baby Jesus cry. And *your* babies are dead because of you. Because you weren't a good daddy."

"Who told you this?"

She giggled again. "Who do you think? My new friend Mickey."

There were no words to describe the look on Weston's face now. Shock, horror, anger, all mixed in with sheer disbelief.

"Mickey?" he said. "Michael *Bonner*?"

"He's the one who told me about you and Kate and Christopher. He knew you were coming this way and he told me how to get you to do exactly what I needed you to."

Weston looked as if he could barely speak. "...How do you even *know* him?"

She giggled again. "That's for me to know and you to find out. But he wants me to deliver a message to you. That's the promise I made. If he helped me kill Kyle and Rebecca, I'd deliver his message."

Weston's whole body went rigid and his lips barely moved. "And what message is that?"

Kate felt her grip tighten on the Beretta and suddenly feared the worst. Had the Beast manipulated this girl—manipulated *her*—into killing Weston? She wanted to scream at Jennifer, beg for her to stop. Tell her that the Beast was a monster, too—just like Kyle and Rebecca—and that she should never have listened to him.

"Mickey says he likes what you're doing. He told me to tell you that."

"Meaning what?"

"Trying so hard to find him. Playing hide and seek." Kate felt herself smile. "He likes playing games. Especially with you. And Christopher."

"You tell him he can go to hell."

"Maybe you can tell him yourself, someday. Because he's out there, Noah. Waiting for you to find him. But he says he won't make it easy for you. Just like in Alabama." Another smile. "Just like right now."

Kate's hand tightened on the grip of the Beretta again, and she thought this was it, that Weston would have to make some quick moves to dodge her fire. But to her surprise she felt herself turning the gun *away* from him.

Bending her elbow, she pressed the muzzle up against her temple, her finger squeezing the trigger...

Weston's eyes went wide as he rushed forward, shouting, "NO!"

He swung the crowbar toward Kate, hitting her gun hand just as the Beretta fired, pain shooting through her wrist as she dropped to the floor...

...and darkness overtook her.

32

KATE AWOKE WITH A START.

She found herself outside the mansion, lying on the concrete next to the pool. Weston was kneeling next to her, shining a flashlight on her. Christopher stood behind him, a small hand resting on Weston's shoulder.

In the dim light, Kate couldn't make out Weston's features well, but she thought she saw wariness in his eyes.

After what'd happened inside the mansion, she wasn't sure she could blame him.

"You all right?" he asked.

She nodded.

I told you she'd be okay.

Kate pushed herself up from the ground and sat. She couldn't remember everything yet, more like vague outlines. But she did remember pulling the trigger on Hoffman's kids.

Or, more accurately, she remembered watching the whole thing unfold, trapped in her own body as a passive observer.

"I shot them both."

It wasn't you, Christopher said. *You had no control over what happened in there.*

"That doesn't make me feel better."

I didn't think it would, but it's the truth. Jennifer wanted this to happen. I'm not sure anything could've stopped her.

Kate nodded slowly. She had a bad case of cottonmouth and her head throbbed. Every move triggered jolts of pain in her muscles and joints. She felt as if she hadn't slept in days. If she didn't know better, she would've guessed she was suffering from a hangover.

"I feel like I was hit by a train," she said.

It's the after effect from having someone—something—else in your body. We probably should get you some food and water.

Kate nodded, suddenly realizing she was ravenous.

"I'm starving," she said.

Another side effect. A possession burns through food.

"Possession?" Kate asked. "You mean like Linda Blair in *The Exorcist?*"

Who?

"You've never heard of Linda—"

"He's eleven," Weston said.

"Right. So if Jennifer possessed me, was she a demon?"

Not a demon. A spirit. Just like you thought. A very angry, determined spirit.

"A ghost?" Kate asked.

They do exist.

"But she's gone now," Weston said. "She was here, looking for revenge, and she got it. Now she's gone. Right, Christopher?"

Yes.

"God, this is all too damn weird," Kate said. "Telepaths who channel spirits of the dead? Now homicidal ghosts."

She looked up at Noah. "Did Jennifer say anything to you while I was unconscious—or whatever the hell I was?"

He shook his head. "Nothing worth hearing."

Kate sensed he was holding something back, but was too exhausted to push the issue. She started to come up from the ground, faltered. Weston reached out, cupped her elbow and rose in tandem with her. A part of her wanted to protest, but her aching joints and weak muscles convinced her to stay quiet and accept his help.

Considering his often gruff, stubborn nature, the gentleness of his touch surprised her.

"Contradictions," Kate said. The word came out as a whisper.

"What?"

"Nothing."

Weston's flashlight beam cast a large circle of yellow light over the concrete. Kate saw a foot protruding from the darkness into the circle. The foot wearing what appeared to be an expensive black pump.

"Lowenthal," Weston said. "She's okay. She'll live. I carried her out, too."

"What about the other two?"

Weston looked at the mansion. "The twins? Neither one of them is going anywhere soon and I didn't feel like sticking around to make sure they don't rise from the dead. Didn't want their crazy to rub off on me."

"Because your life's so sane now."

"Touché."

"Did you call Miller? Agent Page?"

"Knock yourself out. I've had my fill of the FBI. And I'm

guessing we're nowhere near done with them yet."

EPILOGUE

"Half a truth is often a great lie."

~*Benjamin Franklin*

33

THEY WEREN'T DONE WITH THE FEDS.

The FBI took brief statements from Kate and Noah that night before letting them go home for the evening. The following morning, however, agents Page and Jefferson showed up at the motel and put them both through more questioning.

Kate sat across from Agent Page at a small table in her room. The cup of coffee in front of Kate had grown cold and a breakfast bar lay half eaten on a paper napkin next to her drink. A half-empty bottle of water stood on the table in front of Page.

"Lowenthal told me you saved her life," Page said.

"I took two others," Kate replied.

Page's face was stony. "Those two were killers. They were going to kill Lowenthal. They'd already killed Baker. And we found enough evidence in that house to prove they were both behind the Harbinger murders, so they killed their own father, too. I think it was all just a sick game to them. They were probably targeting prostitutes because they're easy to lure and tend to be transient, so nobody really cares."

Kate nodded. She didn't doubt any of that. Just as she didn't doubt that their exposure to the Beast as children had tainted them forever.

Page shuffled through her notes.

"But it does make me curious," she said. "As best we can tell, the two had no history of mental illness. Sergeant Miller volunteered to interview that woman you told us about last night—Barbara Adams—and she says the kids were good, normal children for years, until they changed that one summer. It's like it happened overnight." She paused. "That seems pretty implausible to me. We both know people don't just turn into killers like that."

Kate shrugged. "It's crazy."

"Hoffman's wife passed away a couple of years ago. You knew that, right?"

Kate shook her head.

"Supposedly an accident, but we'll be looking into that, too. Adams said Eva decided against taking the kids back to California because she was afraid that if the judge found out about what had happened to Jennifer, he would've had them jailed or institutionalized. Eva couldn't stand the thought of her precious darlings going through that, so she and Daddy decided they should stay here. That's why Prescott and his people got into the residential property business on such a large scale. When Hoffman came looking for them, and he did several times, they could move from place to place."

"And the woman who probably lost the most out of the deal was helping to hide them by managing the properties.

Before she turned into a lush, at least."

Page nodded. "Adams is a piece of work, all right."

"They killed her kid," Kate said. "And she was scared. They threatened her and sent their enforcer over to constantly remind her of the consequences if she said anything."

"Once the Feds finish investigating Lowenthal's law firm, she may wish they'd killed her, too. It looks like they were protecting Prescott and his people for a very long time. We're looking at multiple prosecutions."

Kate forced a smile. "We can always hope. Will you get that honor?"

"God, I hope not. I hate white-collar crime. That's why I joined VICAP. I'll take a murderous psychopath over a psycho in the executive suite any day of the week. Who knows? Maybe our paths will cross again."

"You and me?" Kate shook her head. "I'm out of the business after this last go around."

Page eyed her from across the table. "Why do I not believe you?"

"Because that's your job," Kate said.

"Because you're not a good liar."

"Do you have any other questions?"

Page nodded. Turning in her seat, she bent down and rummaged through her briefcase for a few seconds. When she came back up, she had a sheet of yellowing paper from a notepad. She laid it on the table, smoothed it down with her palm and slid it across to Kate. On it was a crudely drawn circle with a dot in the center. Page tapped at the symbol with her index finger.

"What is that?" she asked.

"A circle with a dot in it?"

"Is that your final answer?"

"Am I wrong?"

"Technically, I guess not. What else do you know about it?"

"It looks old. Like it was drawn some time ago."

Page grinned and raised an eyebrow at her. "That's it? That's your final answer?"

"What're you, Regis Philbin? Yes. Is that your final question?"

"For now. We found it in the Hoffman kids' papers, along with some old campaign fliers for their grandfather's senate run. I don't know why they decided to use it in that letter they wrote, and at a couple of their crimes scenes, but I have a strange feeling about it. Nothing I can explain. Just a feeling."

Maybe Agent Page had a little psychic ability herself, Kate thought.

"We also found an old satchel in the house. Belonged to Judge Hoffman. Had a bunch of his legal papers in it, along with some newspaper articles about the Harbinger and a handwritten journal that pretty much spelled out his suspicions about his kids. Lowenthal must've gotten a look at it somehow and told Kyle. I'm sure the only reason she was representing Hoffman was to keep an eye on him."

Page leaned forward. Lacing her fingers together, she rested them on the table.

"You realize I'm not stupid."

Kate didn't respond.

"And that we know there's another killer out there."

Kate nodded. "You told me that. But there are a lot of killers out there. And until last night, you thought Noah Weston was one of them. You also thought the judge might be the Harbinger. Turns out you got it *all* wrong, didn't you?"

Page didn't react.

"We could be a lot more effective if we teamed up," she said. "Or, even better, you tell us what you know about this guy," she tapped on the drawing again, "and leave tracking him down to us. You can go off and have a normal life."

A smile ghosted Kate's lips. "Agent Page, I have no idea what you're talking about. But I'm not sure I even know what normal means anymore."

"Now's a good time to find out."

Page picked up the sheet of paper, set it on top of her other documents, slid everything into her briefcase, stood up from her chair, and extended her hand.

Kate stood up and shook it as Page said, "I have a feeling Agent Jefferson hasn't had any better luck with Weston."

"Probably not. If Noah doesn't want to answer, he just doesn't say anything. They could be there for a long time."

Page pulled a business card from the pocket of her jacket and handed it to Kate. "Here's my number. If you think of anything else you'd like to tell me, don't hesitate to call."

"I'll do that," Kate said.

Page grinned. "Somehow, I doubt it. But if you ever get in over your head out there, don't hesitate."

Someone knocked on the adjoining door. Kate went and opened it and found Jefferson waiting on the other side, mopping his forehead with a bright white handkerchief. Jerking a thumb over his shoulder, he said to Page, "Guy's a goddamn monk. I've talked to cement walls that were more forthcoming. You want to give it a shot?"

Page shook her head. "I think we're done here."

Jefferson nodded, then pushed past Kate and joined his partner.

After Kate showed them the door, she headed for Weston's room and found him seated in an armchair, feet propped up on the edge of the bed, studying his fingernails. Christopher sat on the edge of his bed, listening to a game show.

Kate walked over to Weston, who acknowledged her with a nod.

"I got a call from that reporter," she said. "Cindy Davis."

His face brightened. "And?"

"She told me one of the photographers on Prescott's campaign, David Warwick, kept all the negatives for a book. They were lost when a fire destroyed his studio."

Weston's shoulders slumped. "Let me guess. He was in the studio when it happened. What the police call a crispy critter."

"Yes. And the other guy, Jerry Sherman passed away years ago."

"Son of a bitch…"

"We probably shouldn't be surprised," Kate said. "We shouldn't let *anything* surprise us."

"After last night, I won't."

She studied him and frowned. "Is there something you aren't telling me?"

"My partner was possessed by a vengeful spirit and used her as an instrument of revenge. Isn't that enough?"

Kate smirked. "Partner?"

He shrugged and got to his feet. "Not sure what else you'd call it. What do you say we hit the road?"

"The sooner the better. But where to next?"

Weston looked at Christopher, who seemed to have forgotten about his game show and was lost in the haze.

"I guess he'll tell us when he's ready."

We hope you enjoyed this book, and if you did, we'd greatly appreciate a quick review on Amazon, Goodreads and other review sites. And be sure to tell your friends about the book as well. Reader recommendations go a long way toward spreading the word about a good book.

If you have any questions about the Linger Series or any of our other books, feel free to contact us at BraunHaus-Media.com

Thank you.

Robert Gregory Browne
Editorial Director
Braun Haus Media, LLC

www.ingramcontent.com/pod-product-compliance
Lightning Source LLC
Chambersburg PA
CBHW031949170626
46807CB00006B/2413